A Candlelight Ecstasy Romance™

"WHAT MAKES YOU THINK I'M NOT GETTING ALL I BARGAINED FOR?"

He raked her with a flaming glance that said more than words.

"You'll get everything you signed for," she agreed with a calm she was far from feeling. "But that doesn't include me!"

"You're wrong, but we'll go into the details of just how wrong later. Right now I see no reason not to take a small sample of what I've been waiting for during the past month." He drew her closer, ignoring her resistance.

"Take your hands off me!" she blazed.

"I may not have signed anything that guaranteed you'd come to me willingly, but I sure as hell didn't sign anything saying I couldn't take what I wanted!"

CANDLELIGHT ECSTASY ROMANCES™

A
NEGOTIATED
SURRENDER

Jayne Castle

A CANDLELIGHT ECSTASY ROMANCE™

Published by
Dell Publishing Co., Inc.
1 Dag Hammarskjold Plaza
New York, New York 10017

Dell ® TM 681510, Dell Publishing Co., Inc.

Candlelight Ecstasy Romance™ is a trademark of
Dell Publishing Co., Inc., New York, New York.

ISBN: 0-440-16498-2

Printed in the United States of America

First printing—July 1982

Dear Reader:

In response to your continued enthusiasm for Candlelight Ecstasy Romances™, we are increasing the number of new titles from four to six per month.

We are delighted to present sensuous novels set in America, depicting modern American men and women as they confront the provocative problems of modern relationships.

Throughout the history of the Candlelight line, Dell has tried to maintain a high standard of excellence, to give you the finest in reading enjoyment. That is now and will remain our most ardent ambition.

Anne Gisonny
Editor
Candlelight Romances

CHAPTER ONE

"Why are you afraid of me?"

Calla Nevin blinked in barely suppressed astonishment at the outrageous question. There could be only one response, of course. Slanting a pointedly amused blue-green glance up at the man who stood beside her, she lied through her teeth with all the skill at her command.

"I'm not in the least afraid of you. Whatever gave you that idea?"

Slade York leaned negligently against the railing that surrounded the country club pool and half smiled into the velvet darkness of the warm Arizona night. The lights from the club's restaurant and lounge spilled out onto the patio and there was additional discreet lighting hidden in the shrubbery. Enough illumination, in all, for Calla to see the assessing amber of his eyes.

"You, yourself, gave me the idea. Where do you think I got it? You've been nervous all evening. I thought this was supposed to be a celebration and you're acting as if a trap's about to close around your ankle."

The voice was rough and warm and faintly gritty, with an incontrovertible maleness in it that reflected the man.

"I should think I'm entitled to a bit of shaky relief now that the negotiations are over," Calla retorted with a deliberate smile that took a great deal of effort. Her own voice held an almost throaty quality that a man might have been forgiven for finding beguiling. But one look into the cool, aloof blue and green depths of her eyes should have set him straight at once. There was no sultry intention or feminine invitation in those eyes, which watched the

7

world with straightforward interest tinged with a hint of wariness.

"Relief?" Slade's amber-gold eyes, shadowed by long, dark lashes, swept her five feet, four inches of slender, tautly held height, and the half-smile quirked upward in wry mockery.

"I think I'm the one who should be heaving a sigh of relief," he drawled. "You are one tough little bargainer, lady. And to think that when I found out Lester was going to let you handle the negotiations I assumed it would all be a piece of cake."

A quick, annoyed frown flashed across Calla's carefully composed features at his words. She turned her neat head, with its light-brown, bronze-tinted hair drawn into a sleek knot at the nape of her neck, and focused on the swimming pool a few feet away.

"There's no need to tease me, Slade. I'm fully aware of the fact that I was out of my depth. There were times, I think, when you were almost playing with me."

"That's not true, Calla," he denied at once.

She smiled sardonically, both hands in front of her on the railing, and continued to watch the quiet depths of the pool.

"I'm not a fool, Slade. I can only be grateful that you truly wanted to acquire Lester's instrument firm and were willing to pay a fair price for it."

"If I hadn't been willing to pay the price, you would have broken off the negotiations," he reminded her coolly.

She flicked a rueful glance at his harshly hewn face. "Didn't you realize just how desperate Lester was to sell?"

There was a distinct pause while Slade digested the calm remark.

"No," he said at last. "For which he has you to thank. You always acted as if you were dealing from a winning

8

hand and were fully prepared to look elsewhere if you didn't like the way the game was shaping up."

"Thank you." She shrugged one shoulder, which was bared by the deceptively simple black halter dress she wore. "I shall take that as a compliment."

She could feel his restrained aggression as he studied her profile, and Calla knew her own unease was increasing by quantum leaps as the seconds ticked past. How much longer should she delay the inevitable? The negotiations were concluded; all the papers signed and sealed. Her boss, or rather her ex-boss, was enjoying himself thoroughly in the lounge of the country club, pouring champagne and telling guests what a fine job his manager of planning and resources had done. There was no reason to put off telling Slade York her plans, but still she hesitated. He wasn't going to like what she had to say.

The thought of angering this man would probably have made any woman uncomfortable, Calla told herself bracingly. But there really wasn't much he could do to her now. She eyed him speculatively from under her lashes, cataloging the combination of features that produced the sense of latent danger.

He stood about six feet, possibly an inch over. But it wasn't his height that was vaguely intimidating. There were taller men in the world who didn't have the same effect on her. No, it was the lean power in him that made her wary. It wasn't a bulky, muscled strength, but a coordinated, wiry toughness that conveyed leashed energy and supple command.

His conservatively cut hair, not even long enough in back to touch his crisp white collar, was of a darkness the shade of rich roasted coffee beans. Here on the shadowy patio it appeared quite black. The amber eyes flickered as she perused him, and Calla knew Slade was aware of her scrutiny.

He was thirty-seven years old, a fact that Lester Chapman had told her early in the acquisition plans. That gave him seven years of experience on her, Calla had reasoned at the time. Thirty might put her into the "mature woman" category, but she was something of a neophyte in the business world—especially since she had been protected from the hard, street-fighting lessons by the gallant, gentlemanly Chapman.

York could never have been described as a handsome man. The tanned face was far too bluntly carved, with its formidable nose, aggressive jaw, and craggy cheekbones.

He was dressed in the typical casual Phoenix style, wearing dark slacks and a well-tailored jacket over a white shirt. Calla knew without looking that the ever-present leather case in which he carried his dark-framed glasses was in his pocket. The image of him reaching automatically for the case and its contents whenever he was presented with something to read was indelibly printed on her mind. She had seen him do it so often during the past month. . . .

"Do you realize," he inquired on a thread of humor as he broke into her thoughts, "that this is the first time I've seen you in something besides a proper little business suit and appropriate pumps? When you walked in on Lester's arm tonight wearing that long black dress, with your hair sleek and gleaming, more than one man in the crowd decided he needed a manager of planning and resources."

Calla flushed under the unsought compliment and the green in her eyes deepened fractionally.

"It's typical of a man not to appreciate a woman's ability unless it's camouflaged in such a way that it doesn't threaten his sense of superiority!" she snapped without thinking.

"Ouch! I withdraw the comment."

Calla refused to look at Slade. She knew he would be

smiling. Well, that smile wouldn't last long when she divulged her personal plans, she thought grimly.

All the same, she was mildly surprised to hear him attempt the masculine sally. For one thing, she had almost concluded that flattery wasn't his way. He certainly hadn't attempted it during the past month! He had been pure business, and she had been telling the truth earlier when she told him she was experiencing a vast relief tonight. There were times when she'd felt pursued not as a woman but as an opponent, and knowing she had been facing more skilled opposition had made life tense.

There was another reason why his comment had startled her, even as she found it annoying. And that was because Calla knew she was far from being a beautiful woman. He wasn't the first man to have made such a remark, however. Such comments had been coming with greater frequency since her twenty-sixth year, yet they still amazed her. Few people had looked twice at her when she'd entered a room at the age of twenty-two or twenty-three, she reflected with fleeting humor.

It must be that indefinable essence known as experience, she decided. Of course, there was nothing like going through a divorce to give a woman "experience"! By twenty-six the disaster of a marriage was behind her and she had put her life back together again with a single-minded determination that had amazed even herself.

It had been after the divorce that she had discovered ballet lessons as a form of exercise, and the discipline of the dance had invaded her life. She cherished no false illusions of becoming a professional dancer, however, even if it were a remote possibility at her age. No, the rigors of the ballet gave her an inner strength which was infinitely rewarding.

It also had given her a certain presence, and it was this that made men look twice at the thirty-year-old Calla

11

when she entered a room. Her face may have been less than beautiful; although the wide, faintly slanting blue-green eyes were alive with creative reason and, when she was more relaxed, humor. But the poised, controlled manner in which she carried her firm little chin, coupled with her supple posture, gave Calla a vaguely royal air.

Her body was slender, with a high, gentle curve to her breasts and a full flare to her hips. It was a strong body, made so by endless pliés and related exercises. And, she added in amusement, there were her feet. Anyone who took dancing lessons developed very nicely shaped feet and ankles! She wondered if Slade York had noticed them and hid a small grin.

"Are you sleeping with him?" Slade asked after a moment's hesitation.

"What!" Calla swung around to confront him at the softly put question. "This is certainly your night for outrageous comments, isn't it? What sort of impertinent remark is that? And whom, may I ask, are you accusing me of sleeping with?" The line of her throat became longer as she lifted her chin.

He lifted one shoulder indifferently, apparently unconcerned by the warning glitter in her eyes.

"It's an honest question. And I'm referring to your boss. Your ex-boss, that is," he amended with a curious satisfaction. "I suppose I enjoy that title now."

She ignored that, concentrating coldly on the accusation. "I most certainly am not sleeping with Lester Chapman! If I were to tell him what you just asked he'd probably call you out for pistols at dawn! He's a gentleman!"

"I never implied he wasn't," Slade said gently, lifting one coffee-dark brow. "But he's a man . . ."

"Who's old enough to be my father!" she interrupted bluntly.

12

Slade raised a large, square hand placatingly. "Okay, okay. Calm down. I merely asked what a lot of other people probably would if they could."

"What in the world would make people think Lester is my lover?" she bit out. "No, I take that back. I suppose it's a natural assumption, isn't it? I mean, given the fact that people in the business world still have a hard time accepting that a man and a woman can be colleagues!"

"Are you worried that they'll talk about your association with me now?" he inquired a little too mildly.

Calla winced as she realized she had yet to tell him her news. He was still going on the assumption she would be working for him. Well, it was probably safest that way, she decided with a twist of her soft mouth.

"I doubt anyone will have cause to come to any false conclusions about us, Mr. York," she told him repressively. "You strike me as the type of man who will go out of your way to maintain a businesslike air around your employees!"

"Well, I'm not the paternal sort," he admitted dryly.

In spite of herself, Calla knew she was smiling at his tone. "No one would mistake you for a gallant elderly admirer!"

"I trust that was flatteringly meant. What's with the 'Mr. York'? We went on a first name basis the day we were introduced," he added chidingly.

"It was necessary that we communicate as equals," she said lightly. "You made it obvious you were going to address me by my given name so I had no option but to do the same. If I'd continued to refer to you as Mr. York, you might have thought I was demonstrating deference . . ."

"And, thus, weakness?" he chuckled.

"Exactly. I was already working under a disadvantage as it was. I kept telling Lester he needed professionals to

13

handle such a tricky thing as selling a business the size of his."

"But he preferred to leave it in your hands." Slade nodded, his arm resting on the top rail as he continued to lean against the fence. His amber eyes flared warmly over her for an instant, meeting her cool gaze.

"He trusts you implicitly, you know," he said quietly.

"I know. He's been good to me. The best boss I've ever had."

"A hard act to follow, I'll admit. But I'll do my best." Slade smiled, a flash of strong white teeth in the dim light.

Now, Calla thought. *Tell him now. . . .*

"I thought you said you didn't favor the paternal style of management," she heard herself say instead, her slightly husky voice almost bantering.

"I don't, but there are other methods."

"Pity. I've grown rather fond of Lester's style!"

"You'll adapt," he assured her smoothly. "And you needn't worry about not being quite invaluable for some time, you know. You've got a head full of Lester's secrets. You probably know more about the overall workings of the company than anyone who's ever worked there. After his son died . . ."

"Yes, I know." She sighed, remembering how Lester Chapman had been in the process of recovering from his grief when she'd applied for the position of his personal assistant. She had been struggling back from the chaos of divorce and somehow they had found a strange, uncloying comfort in each other. It had developed into a close working relationship, which, in turn, had meant steady advancement for Calla.

"One of the things I was buying when I acquired Lester's firm was your knowledge and insight. I might not have been so tempted to meet your full price if I hadn't known I was getting you in the bargain."

"I'm not part of the inventory, Mr. York," she reminded him stiffly, her eyes back on the pool as she realized how unpleasant life might be when he discovered she wasn't part of the bargain, either.

"As far as I'm concerned you are." He grinned easily. "You'll be managing that branch of my business after tonight. But don't fret, I'll teach you how to run things the way I want them run. I may not have Lester's paternalistic approach but I won't let you flounder for lack of guidance."

"You're too kind," she retorted dryly. "What makes you think I can handle the management of the firm? Up until now I've only handled one section of it!"

"He's taught you the facts of his business. I'll teach you the art of making them work. You've got the technical knowledge and a background in business administration. It's going to work out fine," Slade said with satisfaction.

Calla closed her teeth together with a small snap of barely concealed irritation. Whatever made this man think she was going to work for him? No, that wasn't a fair question, she added instantly as she mentally crossed her fingers. *She'd* made him think she would stay on after Lester left. She'd sensed almost immediately that such assurance was a factor in the negotiations. And she couldn't let Lester down at that point!

"What happens if I turn out to be a slow learner?" she taunted with a brief smile as she glanced up at him inquiringly.

"You forget, I've gotten to know something about your business skills during the past month," he murmured with mocking politeness.

"One can learn a great deal about someone over a bargaining table," she acknowledged feelingly. She had certainly learned very quickly that she wasn't going to find herself working for Slade York when the negotiations were finished!

"What did you find out about me?" he prodded with seemingly cursory interest.

"Is that a serious question or are you making idle conversation?"

"I'm serious," he confirmed, his amber gaze waiting to enmesh her eyes when she turned her head to glance at him. There was a certain watchfulness in him now and Calla felt a tingle along her nerves. "If I said I wasn't serious, though, merely chatting casually, what would you say?"

Her mouth turned upward at the corner in a twist of humor and her eyes laughed at him.

"I'd start by saying that I was tremendously impressed by your knowledge of instrumentation . . ."

"Knowing I own an aviation instrumentation company would make such a remark superfluous," he pointed out.

"But for the purpose of idle conversation that wouldn't matter, would it?"

"Umm, no," he was forced to agree.

"I would then go on to note that you have a definite flair for grasping the essentials of an acquisition package," she continued silkily.

"Thank you," he returned after a moment's close thought. He seemed to decide it was a compliment.

"And then I might say something about your talent for bargaining." She smiled quite innocently.

"Again, thank you. I think." He was still eyeing her skeptically, she noted, waiting for the other shoe to drop.

"Let me see," she mused, tipping her head gracefully to one side. "I suppose I would conclude with some appropriate comment about your straightforward way of dealing."

"A man likes to have others find him honest." He smiled crookedly.

"Yes, it's very useful, isn't it?"

Gold gleamed for a moment in the amber-brown eyes and then Slade said interestedly, "Did you often get sarcastic with Lester?"

"Wouldn't have dreamed of it!"

"Are you trying it out on me because I'm not the paternal sort?"

"Are you implying you don't encourage a free and easy exchange of conversation with your staff?" she asked in liquid accents.

"It occurs to me a little deference might be useful in your case. Perhaps I'll insist you go on calling me Mr. York now that you've reverted to it anyway!"

"You're the boss," she retorted with grave politeness.

"You might try remembering it," he chuckled warmly. "Facing me across a negotiating table has given you ideas, I think."

"Ideas above my station?" She grinned, beginning to regain her courage. After all, there really wasn't anything he could do to her.

"Will it be so hard to go back to the role of employee?" he teased, still holding her eyes with his own.

"I'm very adaptable." *But not that adaptable,* she added silently.

"Good. I'm glad to hear it. Adaptable employees go far in my organization."

"Even the female ones?" She arched an eyebrow.

"Even the female ones. Now, to get back to our conversation . . ."

"Oh, yes. The question of what I learned about you during the bargaining process . . ." She hesitated. "Would you mind telling me what you learned first?"

"What I learned about you? If you like."

She waited with a curious expectancy. What *had* he thought of her during the past few weeks? Had he really respected her abilities or had he been toying with her because he fully intended to buy Chapman's firm in the end and was merely testing her as a future manager?

It was only a matter of idle interest. Regardless of whether or not he had been genuinely impressed with her abilities, she knew what he wanted from her. She'd known it almost from the first, although he had done an admirable job of shielding his goal from Lester and herself. If her own experience hadn't made her so astute where the male of the species was concerned, Calla knew she might not have guessed the masculine drive that was chafing Slade York. Yes, she thought grimly, he had done an excellent job of disguising his aims where she was concerned, and that was going to make him all the angrier when he found out she didn't intend to hang around for the endgame.

"I'll be honest with you," Slade said after a moment, as if he had been seriously considering his answers. "When Lester first introduced us and explained your role it occurred to me he might be trying to . . ."

"Use a very ancient tactic?" Calla suggested coolly.

"Well, yes. It wouldn't be the first time a woman has been used as a pawn to weaken a man."

Slade shifted as he said the words, giving her a very direct, very hard look that she met with outward poise. He was somehow closer now, having shortened the distance between them without appearing to do so in an obvious way. She was aware of the lean hardness in him and of the intent that seemed to emanate from the lithe body. Had he really thought he could hide his motives from her? Men like this were so easy to understand now. Too bad she hadn't been so bright when she was twenty-five.

"I'm sure Lester knew such a diabolical scheme would

never have succeeded with you," she told him with an artificially sweet smile.

His gold eyes narrowed dubiously. "Are you sure you never talked to your old boss that way?"

"There was never any need."

"Lester always stayed in his place?" he asked interestedly.

"Lester, as I've mentioned, is a gentleman!"

"I could take that as an insult, I suppose," he remarked as if thinking about it.

"Please don't. I'm dying to hear the rest of your observations at the negotiating table." *Before I reveal my own and end the evening,* she finished wryly in her mind.

He watched her for a moment longer, his gaze hooded, and she wondered for the first time if he suspected what was coming. Then he appeared to capitulate graciously, a serious expression shaping the hard line of his mouth.

"I learned," he said slowly, "that you are a very loyal manager of planning and resources. There was no doubt at any time during the past month about your dedication to achieving the best possible deal for your firm . . . even when I, uh, hinted that there might be something in it for you if you backed off a few of your demands."

Calla drew a deep breath. "So I didn't imagine those hints?"

"No."

"Would you have made good on the implied promises if I had backed down on a couple of occasions?" She tried to view him clinically, noting the tightening lines at the corner of his lips and the fine tension marks around his eyes. He was just like all the others. Smarter than many of them, to be sure, but essentially just the same.

"Oh, yes," he confirmed immediately. "I would have made good on the hints. But to tell you the truth, I wasn't particularly sorry to see you stick by your guns. Loyalty is an invaluable commodity these days, and while one doesn't expect to find it very often, when it occurs a man would be a fool not to appreciate it."

"I see," she said evenly. "Your appreciation was completely altruistic, then? You were glad your good friend and fellow businessman Lester Chapman had enjoyed the benefit of a totally loyal member of management for the past four years?"

For a moment she thought he was going to censure her thinly veiled sarcasm again but all he said was "A successful businessman is seldom altruistic, Calla. I was glad to see your capacity for loyalty because I knew you would soon be working for me."

"And you think such loyalty can be easily transferred?" She smiled inquiringly.

"I think in this case it had better be," he growled on a deep laugh. "I certainly paid a high enough price for it!"

Calla bit back a sharp retort. "What else did you learn about me?"

"That you come to a meeting fully prepared. That you're organized and efficient and that you have a great deal of self-discipline," he summarized matter-of-factly.

"Praise indeed! I must have given you a better deal than I thought."

"You didn't give anything away, if that's what you're worried about. But I'm satisfied."

He gave a short nod as he said the words as if emphasizing the fact that he was content with the deal he had just concluded.

"It's your turn," he reminded her, pushing aside his unbuttoned jacket to rest one large fist on his narrow hip as he continued to lounge against the rail. He waited with a kind of reined-in aggression.

"What did I learn about you?" She repeated the initial question thoughtfully, knowing the moment would soon be upon her and steeling herself for the final confrontation. "I learned that you're as organized, efficient, and self-disciplined as you just said I am," she replied. "I also learned a great deal more. I know you're capable of a certain ruthless determination, a driving desire to make things go your way, and that you take pleasure in controlling your environment and the people in it. You're quite single-minded when you set your sights on an objective and you're devoted to the art of the successful maneuver. In short, Mr. York, you're the quintessential business-man."

She was no longer looking at him, her glittering eyes focused once more on the shimmering pool. But she could feel his sudden stillness beside her and knew he was scenting trouble. When he spoke there was a new chill in his tone.

"I'm lost for words. You'll have to clarify your comments a bit further. Were they compliments or accusations?"

"What do you think?" she challenged softly.

"I'm beginning to think they might have been accusations," he admitted dryly.

"They were statements of fact, Mr. York."

"Mr. York?" he repeated, the grittiness of his voice more pronounced. "Are you going to insist on addressing me that way because you now work for me?"

"No," she responded with false ease, drawing a deep breath and turning lightly on her heel to face him. The long black dress swished softly around her ankles.

"I've taken to calling you Mr. York this evening because it's a useful way of putting some formality into the situation."

"And why do we need formality at this point?" he charged softly.

She could feel all of his senses come alert and knew he

21

was instinctively preparing for battle even though he couldn't yet know what she was about to do.

"Because I'm going to tell you that I've decided not to be a part of the acquisition package. The inventory you just purchased from Lester Chapman includes a lot of instruments but not a manager of planning and resources."

She waited with her regal head held high, her eyes clear and determined, while the silence between them lengthened dangerously. She knew he was running through a variety of approaches before selecting the one with the most steel in it, and she tensed herself for the slice of the razor.

The amber and gold eyes hardened into a tempered alloy as he watched her calm, composed features in the shadowy light. He didn't move from his casual position but Calla felt as if he had gathered himself to spring.

"You were part of the deal. You know that."

The words were soft, devoid of any emotion whatsoever. And that made them all the more menacing.

"I know you chose to believe I was going to stay with the firm after the sale but I never said as much, nor did I sign any contract to that effect."

"You allowed both Lester and myself to think you were more than eager to stay on. Neither he nor I saw any need to put it in writing."

Calla touched the tip of her tongue to the edge of a dry lower lip and quickly cursed herself for the small betrayal of tension. "I know what you believed."

"Because you engineered those beliefs?"

She didn't deny it. There was nothing she could say. She had deliberately allowed him to think what he wished.

"Why?" It was a blunt, no-nonsense question and, perhaps, she decided honestly, it deserved an answer.

"I knew you wanted me," she said simply.

"There was never any doubt about that. You are an extremely valuable asset. As I said before, you've got a head full of Lester's secrets and those secrets are going to be very, very useful in the coming months."

"No," she said very carefully, quite softly, "I wasn't referring to that. I knew you . . . *wanted* me."

There was a short, incredibly charged second of silence. Calla stood with unconscious dignity, her fingers clenched into the wooden rail beside her. She tried to imagine it as a barre such as she used in ballet class and deliberately tried to relax her fingers to the proper degree of tension. It was an interesting exercise but not especially effective in relieving the tautness of the moment.

"Ah," he breathed finally. "I understand. Now *that* I thought I *had* kept from you during the negotiations." He inclined his head once in a small gesture of mocking admiration. "My congratulations. You are even more astute than I had given you credit for." There was a slight pause and then he said, "It changes nothing, of course. You're still coming to me as part of the bargain we have concluded for Lester's firm."

Calla stared at him, a little shocked in spite of herself at the casual certainty he was exhibiting.

"You don't seem to comprehend, Mr. York," she said, summoning a brilliantly frosty smile. "I wouldn't work for you if you were the last man on earth paying above minimum wage!"

Calla whirled and walked away from him. The endgame had been short, she decided, but very final.

CHAPTER TWO

Calla got precisely three steps before the ruthless fingers closed around her arm, bringing her to an abrupt halt.

"Not so fast, my conniving little negotiator," Slade muttered with soft menace. He pulled her around to face him, his hand clamped on her like the jaws of a trap.

"There's nothing you can do," she assured him haughtily. "The deal is closed. You are now the proud owner of an instrument firm and you can't very well give it back to Lester!"

"I have no intention of trying to back out of the bargain. You've seen to it that it was well and truly sealed, haven't you?" he grated.

"I did my best," she acknowledged politely.

"What makes you think I'm not going to get all that I bargained for?" He raked her with a flaming glance that said more than words.

"You'll get everything you signed for," she agreed with a calm she was far from feeling. "But that doesn't include me!"

"No?"

"No!"

"You're wrong, but we'll go into the details of just how wrong later. Right now I see no reason not to take a small sample of what I've been waiting for during the past month!"

He used the single hand on her bare arm to draw her closer, ignoring her resistance.

"Take your hand off me!" she blazed tightly, the blue-green of her eyes full of the cold of an arctic sea.

"I may not have signed anything that guaranteed you'd

come to me willingly but I sure as hell didn't sign anything saying I couldn't take what I wanted!"

He was angry, she knew. Angrier than she had expected. But she, of all people, should have known how fragile were the egos of men like this. Calla put out a hand in futile protest, wedging it against his chest as she was crushed ruthlessly into the heat and power of his body.

There was a disorienting combination of sensations. She felt the strength of his thighs as she was hauled against them; the singularly male scent of him filled her nostrils and the steel in his arms as they closed around her was enough to take away her breath.

Before she could sort out the different aspects of the overwhelming assault, his mouth came down on hers with a predatory savagery that locked any words of protest in her throat.

At first the anger in him fed on her lips, taking without restraint and forcing the delicate skin on the inside of her mouth harshly against her teeth.

His tongue emerged to plunge into the warmth behind her lips, stalking the honey there the way a ravaging bear would have taken it from a hive. And he was as heedless of the threat of bee stings as the bear would have been. When she attempted to retaliate by closing her teeth warningly on his invading tongue he withdrew for an instant and used his own teeth almost but not quite painfully on her full lower lip.

"Oh!" She gasped at the unexpected shock and then he was back inside her mouth, secure in the knowledge that he'd crushed her poor attempt at defense.

Her fingers curled like small claws into his shoulder but the violence was deflected by the thickness of his jacket. Desperately, as she felt him begin to consolidate and pursue his attack, Calla sought for a way of dealing with it. It was like trying to think of a battle strategy after the enemy had already begun shelling. Her options were limited and she finally settled on the old but effective one of complete passiveness.

She felt the kiss continue to explode, threatening to consume her in the heat and fire of male domination. His hands slid down the length of her back to her hips, propelling her into an intimate contact that seemed to burn through the fabric of the black dress.

"Such a firm, straight little back," Slade breathed against her cheek as he finally released her captured mouth to explore the new territory. "When I saw you dancing earlier with Chapman and he put his fingers here . . ."

One of his hands moved again to stroke the length of naked spine revealed by the halter dress and Calla shivered in reaction. It was like having a delicate electrical charge applied to her skin.

"When he put his hands on you like that I wanted to chase out onto the dance floor and pull you out of his arms! But I figured I'd been patient for a month, I could afford to wait a little longer. How was I to know you were planning to run!"

"I'm not running!" she managed to protest, standing very still in the fierce embrace, aware of his feathering kisses on her eyelids as he sensed her lack of resistance. He was unleashing the primitive, punishing aggression now that she'd ceased fighting him. His kisses were turning languid and provocatively persuasive. For some strange reason she had become aware of the hard edge of his eyeglass case digging into the softness of her small, unconfined breasts. With all the other tactile sensations impinging on her, she didn't know why that one stood out.

"Don't deny it! You just told me you were planning on leaving the company now that the acquisition had gone through! But it's too late for flight, Calla. If you were

27

intent on escape, you should never have seen the negotiations through to the end!"

She felt his breath warm and slightly deepened as he grazed little gnawing kisses along her cheekbone to the tip of her ear. Her eyes closed in a blind denial even as she felt another tremor course through her.

"There's nothing you can do, Slade," she reminded him fiercely, her voice barely above a whisper. "I'm not going to work for you. I refuse to work for a man who is as ruthless and domineering as you are. Especially when that man has decided he wants me! We couldn't possibly have a decent working relationship!"

"If we have to choose, ultimately, between a working relationship and the other kind of relationship, then I'll accept your resignation. But in the meantime I think we can have both," he declared with rumbling arrogance.

"You're out of your mind!" she stormed furiously, her eyes opening wide for an instant to meet his as he lifted his head.

"You think so?" She could sense the mocking amusement in him as his eyes gleamed down into her angry, upturned features.

"I find the thought of giving you an occasional dressing down during the day rather intriguing, knowing as I will that I'll be undressing you later that night!" His smile was one of anticipation and menace.

"You insufferable, arrogant fool! I hope for your sake you didn't buy Lester's firm for the purpose of acquiring me!"

He smiled at that—almost whimsically, she thought wretchedly.

"Sweetheart," he murmured on a hint of laughter, "I want you very badly, but there are other means of acquiring a woman than by purchasing an entire company!"

"You'll certainly have to find them if you intend to have me!"

That last bit of bravado was a foolish challenge that Calla instantly regretted. But, damn him! He was behaving with such classic male certainty that she found herself retaliating in kind!

He grinned. "When did you decide to run, Calla Nevin? Did you know that I wanted you the first day I met you? Or was it something you realized as the negotiations progressed?"

He was still holding her against him, his arms locked around her waist, as he waited for an answer.

"I knew I wasn't going to work for you the first day I met you," she was goaded into saying. "But it wasn't because I realized you were intending to drag sex into the matter. It was because I have a built-in dislike of men who wield power the way you do. As if it were yours by divine right!"

"Wait a minute," he growled feelingly, his eyes narrowing. "I behaved very well for the past few weeks! I didn't yell or rage or bang my fist on the table. Whatever gave you the impression I'm some kind of domineering slave-driver?"

"Your reputation preceded you," she told him with exquisite sweetness.

"But Lester likes me! He wouldn't have given you a bad impression!" Slade protested irritably.

"He didn't."

"Then how . . ."

"Do you think I would have entered into such delicate negotiations without having you thoroughly checked out?" Her arched brow mocked him.

"My God!" he muttered in a combination of wonder and astonishment. "Did Lester know?"

"I saw no reason to tell him. I found out nothing that

29

made you a poor prospect as a buyer. And, to tell you the truth, we didn't have that many would-be buyers panting on our doorstep!"

"So you detached your personal feelings and went ahead with the project." He nodded, looking fascinated. "In spite of the fact that you concluded I'm ruthless, arrogant, and domineering."

"You also had the capital to invest in Lester's business!" she reminded him spiritedly.

"The deciding factor?"

"I'm afraid so."

"What was it in my murky background that convinced you I'd make such an intolerable boss?" he demanded, heavy brows drawing together in an intimidating frown.

"You're intolerant." She tossed his own word easily back at him.

"Only of incompetence!"

"Your temper is famous among the members of your staff."

"No one's ever quit because I lost my temper with him or *her!*" he stated righteously.

"Agreed. That's because, being a man, a certain amount of violent temper is considered acceptable in you. But it's not acceptable to me."

"I am *never* violent," he gritted between clenched teeth.

"That's a matter of opinion. My arm still hurts where you grabbed me a few minutes ago!"

"Please continue with the list of my inadequacies," he ordered in velvet tones, "as I do not intend to apologize for restraining you. I was under pressure."

"Under pressure is when a good boss should be able to control himself!"

"As long as he can control others, it's unimportant how he reacts! Now go on with the list!" Slade ordered tersely, still holding her close to his body with a grip of iron.

"There was the way you acquired that small firm two years ago," Calla went on seethingly. "It was a takeover of the most unfriendly kind!"

"There was a reason for that. . . ."

"I know. You wanted the firm. You seem to have a way of getting what you want!" she snapped.

"Remember that!" He appeared to relent as soon as the warning was uttered because his face softened slightly as he went on in more soothing tones. "About that other acquisition . . . Matheson was a crook, Calla. He deserved everything he got."

"You have a reputation of being unable to sustain long-term relationships," Calla went on feelingly, determined to pursue the list.

"What's that supposed to mean?" he demanded belligerently.

"You know damn well what it means! You've had a string of women a mile long since your divorce a few years ago!" Good Lord! What had made her say that?

"That doesn't need an excuse except the obvious!" he thundered, glaring down at her.

"You mean the fact that you're a man?" she clarified a little too gently.

"Yes! But don't stop there. Are you going to hold my divorce against me, too?" he invited with clear, anticipatory menace.

"I can't," she informed him briskly, wishing she'd held her tongue. "I've got one behind me, too."

"I know," he said with satisfaction. "I was going to bring that little fact up if you didn't!"

"How did you know about it?" she grumbled, feeling on the defensive.

"Lester told me. Said you'd arrived on his doorstep four years ago so full of guts and determination to start a new

31

life that he found himself hiring a personal assistant he could have sworn he didn't need."

Calla flushed. "He had no right . . ."

"Take it up with him."

"We're straying from the subject," she pointed out imperiously.

"Go ahead, tell me the other reasons you don't think you can work for me," he muttered.

"Haven't I made it plain? I don't approve of your business practices and I don't admire the way you run your personal life, although I freely admit that's none of my business. And, on top of all that, I couldn't possibly work for a man who has the incredible arrogance to think that he was buying a new mistress when he bought Lester's company! Besides," she couldn't help adding with a certain relish, "you wouldn't like the way I managed your new branch, anyhow!"

For some reason that seemed to startle him. "Why not? You'll manage it the way I teach you to manage it."

"Perhaps five or six years ago, Slade York, you could have molded me into the sort of employee you want. But not today. I have my own style, and while I'm more than willing to learn, I have no intention of making myself over into someone else's image. Especially when that image involves becoming another one of your women! It would be an impossible working situation."

"You're intelligent enough to adapt to my way of doing things . . ." he began forcefully, amber eyes slitting.

"I may be intelligent enough, but I'm not cooperative enough," she stated simply. "I have no intention of changing myself to suit any man."

"Is that why your husband left you?" he grated.

Calla whitened, but her voice, when she replied, was steady. "I do not discuss that with anyone."

His mouth tightened and for an instant she thought

there was indecision in him, an unfamiliar reaction from Slade York. The man was never indecisive. Then he had the grace to look a little apologetic. "I'm sorry. That was not a fair comment. You do have a way of provoking me, sweetheart."

"Don't call me that."

She stepped backward determinedly and, to her private relief, he let her go. She faced him from the small distance, her head high, her eyes proud and faintly contemptuous.

"I believe that concludes our little discussion, Mr. York. If you don't mind, I'm going back inside to find Lester. I intend to leave."

He watched her thoughtfully. "You can't." The words were simple and to Calla's ears had a horribly final sound to them.

"Watch me." She smiled grimly and swung around to make her exit.

Unfortunately, even as she was congratulating herself on the termination of the scene, the whole situation was thrown into mild chaos at the sight of Lester Chapman coming through the open sliding glass windows, a beaming look of approval on his handsome, middle-aged face. His wealth of silver hair gleamed in the faint light and his faded blue eyes smiled at Calla as he came forward.

"So this is where you two disappeared! Have I interrupted a meeting of a mutual admiration society? Are you both telling each other what brilliant negotiators you are?" He put a familiar arm around Calla's shoulders and aimed his perceptive blue gaze at Slade, who was frowning.

"Not exactly," Slade said dryly, his gold eyes raking the picture Calla made under Chapman's casual embrace. "Calla has just been telling me why she can't possibly stay on after you leave."

"What?" Lester glanced inquiringly down at her stiffly

held figure. "I thought you wanted to remain, Calla? Slade's counting on you to help in the transition process, at least."

"Oh, Slade's counting on much more than that," Calla said coolly.

"I detect a loaded remark," Lester said quietly, his eyes on her face.

"Ask Slade. I find myself bored with the discussion."

Without another word, Calla slipped out from under his arm and concluded her retreat, leaving the two men together on the patio. She had a last glimpse of Lester standing there, perplexed, and Slade watching her with a certain frustration, and then she was back inside the crowded country club lounge.

"I see you've lost your bodyguard for the evening," said a pleasant male voice at her elbow. "Can I convince you to go out on the dance floor with someone besides Chapman?"

Calla summoned a smile for the good-looking man with the curly blond hair and the open, cheerful features. "Thank you, Boyd, I'd love it."

"Great. I thought I'd never get my chance." He led her out onto the floor, taking her into his arms in a conventional fashion and smiling down at her with warm, hazel eyes. Boyd Carson worked for Lester's recently sold business. If she had elected to stay on and work for Slade, Calla would have been the young man's boss. She wondered if he would still have asked her to dance if he'd known York's plans. Men were at their most charming with women who didn't represent a threat to their egos. Nice as he was, she was certain Boyd was no different from the others.

"This whole thing has gone rather smoothly, hasn't it?" Boyd was saying chattily as he steered her around the floor. "The staff always worries a bit when they learn their

34

company is being sold. Work-force reductions, changes in benefits, responsibilities, things like that. But after that statement was issued guaranteeing no one was going to lose a job because of the sale, everyone settled down. That was a smart move on York's part. It got the staff on his side immediately."

Calla quirked her lips slightly, wondering what Boyd would say if he knew she'd been the one to insist on that statement being issued. Slade hadn't wanted to do it, claiming he wanted the freedom to get rid of "dead wood." But Calla had stood firm and he'd finally agreed. She had convinced him that the ensuing good will was worth more than the threat of inefficiency. Inefficiency could be dealt with in other ways. Not that Slade was familiar with other methods of management. His instinctive response to most business situations was the most ruthless and effective one he could find. She tensed at the thought.

"Any idea what your role will be now that Chapman's leaving?" Boyd went on conversationally. "Will you stay on in your present position as manager of planning and resources?"

"No, I don't think so," she said politely. "As a matter of fact, I plan to . . ."

Her words were cut off as a large hand descended on her bare wrist.

"Mind if I cut in, Carson?"

"Of course not, Mr. York," Boyd said swiftly, ingratiatingly. He released Calla with what she could only describe as embarrassing alacrity.

"Don't think too harshly of him," Slade advised, sweeping her into a much closer embrace than Boyd had attempted. "He knows which side his bread is buttered on! And I do have to talk to you."

"Boyd's willingness to let you take over his partner on

35

the dance floor doesn't surprise me in the least. He has no intention of offending the new president of the company!"

"Too bad you don't share his sentiments. It would make things less volatile," Slade commented broodingly.

"When I'm out of the picture I'm sure you'll find matters quite easy to manage. I'm doing you a favor, you know," she added brightly, a very winning sort of smile on her face that had nothing to do with the cool sea color in her eyes.

"A favor! How the hell do you figure that?"

"It's simple. I know you think you know what you want."

"*Think* I know . . . !" he started, and she could sense the muffled explosion he was stifling.

"Men always think they know what they want. They're like children who see a bright, shiny toy and decide to have it for their own. In this case you've convinced yourself that you want me. Two things will happen now that I'm moving the toy out of reach."

"I'm not sure I want to hear this," he growled, amber eyes staring at her in disbelief. "I've always avoided the type of female who took just enough psychology in college to be dangerous!"

Calla's smile broadened. "Would you rather not hear the rest of my analysis?"

"You know I have no choice. I have to figure out what's motivating you and that means I have to know what you think is motivating me! God! I'm beginning to sound like you!"

"Don't worry. A little self-reflection is good for the soul. As I was saying, as I move the toy—myself—out of reach you'll go through two stages."

"I'll cry?" he suggested hopefully.

"Not at all. You'll decide you want me more than ever. I shall move into the category of challenge. If I were to

36

surrender at that point, you would find the challenge conquered. Your ego would be satisfied, and after a time you would go on to other interests. If I don't surrender you will begin to switch from seeing me as a challenge to resenting me. You will eventually convince yourself you don't want me after all and you will go on to other interests. Either way, it's the same result," she concluded with a small lifting of one shoulder. "You can't blame me for preferring the latter route of arriving at that result. Much easier on *me!*"

"Fascinating. But what happens if I don't fall into that pattern? What happens if I lose my head completely and fall in love with you?"

"I doubt that's much of a viable possibility, given your track record with women. I believe I mentioned earlier that you don't seem inclined to form long-term relationships."

"But if it were to happen?" he insisted, his gritty voice tantalizing and slightly urgent.

"If it were to happen," she repeated obligingly, her own husky tones hardening as she confronted his amber gaze with absolute certainty, "then a slight variation on the pattern would develop. If you were to fall in love, then, for a time, you would naturally see everything about me through a rosy haze, including my career. You would probably even be proud of me and that emotion might last indefinitely. Until, that is, the career became a threat to you."

"Hah!" he interrupted, appearing enormously pleased with himself. "How could your career threaten me?

"You think that because you would be my boss you would always be safely in the dominant position?" she mocked. "I've got news for you. A lot can go wrong with that scenario. The most obvious, naturally, is that I reach a point where I've gone as far as I can with your firm and

I decide to go to work for someone else. If I became too successful under another man's influence you would begin to resent it. On top of that, I'm at a point now where I already do a certain amount of traveling for the company. Even if I were to remain with the firm, I have a hunch those important little out-of-town trips to sales conferences and state-of-the-art seminars would quickly cease. Men get very nervous when the women they love travel on business."

"There's a good reason for that," he retorted at once, frowning severely. "Those conferences are still largely male-oriented and a woman alone . . ."

"Without the protection of her lover?" she murmured encouragingly, looking up at him with wide, innocent eyes.

"Yes, dammit! A woman traveling to one without the protection of a man is going to face a lot of difficulties."

"You mean a lot of *temptation*, don't you?" she smiled sweetly.

"You're deliberately trying to set me up," he accused flatly, his hand on her naked back tightening perceptibly.

"I'm trying to point out the impossibility of us working together now that you've convinced yourself you want me! Men like you are possessive, arrogant, and demanding. While they're involved with a woman they have to dominate the arrangement or they turn resentful and sulky. Eventually they seek another woman who doesn't pose a threat to their egos. It's all very simple and straightforward, really."

"You sound as if you've been through it before," he noted coldly.

"I have. Four years ago. I do not intend to go through it again."

"Well, we're progressing at least," he suddenly sighed, humor edging his mouth. "Out there on the patio you refused to discuss your former husband. Now you've just finished telling me why your marriage broke up!"

Calla stared at him, at first stunned and then infuriated by how easily he had dragged the bare outlines of the story out of her. And she had fallen into the trap like a willing victim.

Without a word, she pulled free of his hold and came to a halt. "I assure you, you know nothing about me or my past. But I have no intention of standing here and brawling with you over the subject. I'm leaving."

"If you're going to follow through on your earlier announcement that you were going to have Lester drive you home, forget it. I've already told him I'll be taking you home this evening. He was more than willing to give up the privilege," Slade murmured from behind her as he followed her off the dance floor. "I think he rather likes the idea of a romance between the two of us. A way of keeping the company 'in the family,' as it were."

"That's ridiculous. I'm not a member of his family," Calla said waspishly as she walked gracefully toward Lester's table. The older man smiled genially as he watched her approach.

"I think you've come to fill the role of daughter during the past four years." Slade's arm came around her waist as if he were guiding a willing woman off the floor.

"I thought you'd decided he was my lover!"

"I've changed my mind after talking to him. He's not going to let you leave me flat, you know. Just thought I'd warn you."

Calla was unable to respond to the taunting statement because Lester was already rising to seat her beside him.

"Did the two of you work things out?" he demanded cheerfully as he politely held Calla's chair.

"She hasn't started the negotiating process yet." Slade

grinned, taking the seat across from the other two. "I'm being kept on tenterhooks."

"I'm not going to stay on, Lester," Calla said quietly but with great conviction. "York Instruments doesn't need me. I'm sure Slade will find himself quite capable of managing his new acquisition without my assistance." She refused to meet the amber gaze across the table.

"Calla," Lester said slowly, carefully, "I can see you're pretty determined about this, but, well, frankly, I more or less gave Slade to understand that your abilities would be there at least during the transition process."

Calla looked at him helplessly. "I'm sorry if you made any statements to that effect, Lester . . ."

"He did more than that," Slade announced coolly. "He gave me his word on it. We shook hands over the deal."

"I told you, I'm not part of the inventory!" she hissed, her gaze lifting to clash with his.

"The secrets in your head most certainly are part of the inventory I just purchased," Slade told her uncompromisingly. She saw once again the flash of the steel in him that she had seen so often during the past month.

"It's true, Calla," Lester said softly, regretfully. "I'm sorry, my dear, but I honestly thought you wanted to stay on. I had no idea . . ."

"I saw the final papers before they were signed and I read them thoroughly. There's no mention of me in them!" she shot back with grim triumph.

"This was a . . ." Lester hesitated, searching for the right word. "A gentleman's agreement, I'm afraid."

"How can that be when there was only one gentleman involved?" she muttered. "It takes two to form an agreement!"

"Calla!" Lester looked a trifle shocked. "I assure you, Slade is a man of his word! You have no reason to insult him."

Instantly Calla backed off the hasty statement, mentally chastising herself for having let her temper run away with her tongue. "I know the two of you are friends, Lester, but I . . ."

"Let's forget the rest of the arguments in favor of you letting down your former boss and just stick to the matter at hand, shall we?" Slade interrupted coldly. "Are you or are you not going to assist during the transition?"

"I have no desire to work for you, Slade York! Can't you comprehend that?" she demanded fiercely, keenly aware of Lester regarding her with a hurt expression. He had been so good to her during the past four years. She had become an important force in the day to day running of his firm. He *counted* on her!

"I understand. That doesn't answer my question."

There was a moment of tension during which Calla felt the impact of the combined will of the two men. If it had been only Slade's wishes involved she would have been able to ignore the whole thing and walk out the door. But Lester seemed so distraught. . . . Had he really envisioned her as a daughter to whom he was leaving the business?

"Calla, please," the older man said quietly. "Just for a few months. Your experience would be invaluable and there is so much Slade has to learn about our employees and the way we manage things . . ."

He let the sentence trail off suggestively and Calla knew he was resorting to another sort of appeal. Lester was subtly warning her that if she didn't stay on to supervise the transition, Slade would have a free rein. She shivered at the thought of him descending on Chapman, Inc. with no one to moderate his natural ruthlessness. How could she even be sure he would honor the statement he had made about not letting any of the "dead wood" go if she wasn't on the scene?

All this she saw in Lester's faded blue gaze as she sat very still. That feeling of being pursued returned and she wanted to shout her defiance of the man who was calmly maneuvering her in the direction he wanted.

"Lester?" she whispered tentatively.

"I promised him, Calla. I give you my word."

She continued to stare at him for another agonizing moment, knowing full well she should be putting herself first this time, not her ex-boss. There was a danger in staying near the source of the new power in her life. She should be running a million miles in the opposite direction. . . .

Coldly, eyes narrowed, she turned to meet the watchful look in Slade's golden gaze. He was waiting with cool, predatory patience. He knew she had no choice.

"How long?" she asked in a hard whisper.

"Six months," he returned unhesitatingly. They were back to facing each other across a negotiating table.

"One month," she snapped instantly. "Six months is absolutely out of the question. There's no need. I can teach your new manager whatever he or she needs to know in one month."

"Perhaps. If I had that new person ready to step into your shoes. But I don't because I was under the impression you'd be the one taking over the job. It will take me at least six months to find and train someone new."

"You'll have to work a good deal faster than that!" she vowed.

He eyed her narrowly. "All right, I'll cut it down to four. On the understanding that I can find someone within the next few weeks. If that doesn't work out, I'll need the full six months."

"You'll get three months from me whether or not you're successful in recruiting a new manager. That's my final offer. I simply won't commit myself to any more time." She sat back in her chair, challenging him to argue.

He gave her a level stare as if considering her ultimatum and then he appeared to make his decision.

"All right," he agreed bleakly. "Three months it is."

There was a charged silence around the table as the three people present considered what had just taken place, and then Lester smiled broadly and winked at Calla. "You know, you two are a treat to watch. I've thoroughly enjoyed myself during the past month and tonight was a fitting ending!"

"Lester," Calla began, determined to ignore his delight in the way things had worked out, "if you don't mind I would like to go home."

"Didn't Slade tell you?" Lester said gently. "He's volunteered to take you home. Which leaves me free to stay here a while longer yet. You know how it is at parties like this. I'm a born socializer!"

Slade was already getting to his feet. "Let's go, Calla. It will be my pleasure to see my newest manager safely home."

CHAPTER THREE

"That little rebellion was certainly squashed easily enough." Slade grinned in satisfaction as he gently stuffed Calla into his silver Mercedes. "Are you always going to be this amenable?"

Calla shot him a scathing glance as he slid in beside her and started the engine. "Are you being deliberately offensive or do you just naturally have to crow whenever you get your own way?"

"I suppose it is rather unfair to enjoy such an easy victory. You must really have a soft spot in your heart for Chapman! You didn't put up much of a fight at all when he looked at you with that fatherly gaze and asked you to stay on for the sake of the business!"

She knew he was teasing her and would have given a great deal in that moment to get her own back. The mocking grin still curved his mouth and his craggy profile was set in the lines of masculine satisfaction.

"I hope you realize," she told him in a cool, silky voice, "that the agreement we just reached will be completely null and void if you so much as put a hand on me."

"I've already put a hand on you," he pointed out imperturbably. "But if you're worried about me mixing business and pleasure—don't. I wouldn't think of causing a lot of office gossip at work. However, after work is our own time, and I . . ."

"The clause applies to after work as well!" she snapped quickly.

"Then you should have made it part of the original agreement we reached back there at the country club," he chuckled. "You negotiated in haste, little one, and now you're stuck with the terms of the deal. For *Lester's* sake, of course!"

"Doesn't it bother you at all to resort to deliberately using a person's weak point?" she asked with a fair imitation of detached interest. She watched his competent handling of the wheel and the casual alertness of his driving as if she were studying an alien life form.

"Why should it? What's the point of dragging out a situation when it can be quickly finalized and the arrangement implemented?"

"And you wonder where you got your reputation for being ruthless!" she muttered tightly, turning to watch the palm trees that lined the street. It was getting late but there was still enough moon out to distinguish some of the jagged peaks of the mountains that encircled Phoenix.

He arched an eyebrow in arrogant humor. "What makes you think I wondered about that? Don't forget, by the way, you're supposed to be giving me driving directions."

Calla sighed in disgust and rattled them off. What was she getting so upset about, anyway? The man was annoying in the extreme, but hadn't she just spent a month proving she could handle him? True, she had been nervous, with a distinct feeling of being out of her league, but, ultimately, she had engineered good terms and there had been several occasions when she'd made Slade York back down. She could handle him. And she could handle the next three months, too, she told herself bracingly. Lester had been right in the implication that it would be better to have someone on the scene to prevent York from running roughshod over his new staff.

Under Calla's terse instructions, Slade found the sleek, modern Spanish-style condominium complex in the quiet Phoenix suburb and pulled into the parking lot with an approving nod.

"A nice place," he said, opening her car door a moment later. "Looks like you, in a way. Style combined with warmth."

Calla flashed a startled sideways glance at him as he walked her toward the door. "There's no warmth in me for you, Slade. Don't waste your time kidding yourself!"

"There's plenty of heat under the surface of that cool exterior of yours, Calla Nevin," he told her almost roughly. "And I'm going to . . ."

He broke off as they came to a halt in front of her door, his amber eyes glaring at the array of flowers sitting on the mat. A card dangled invitingly from the bouquet.

"What the hell is that?" he demanded accusingly.

"Well, I can't be positive, naturally, but at a rough guess, I'd say someone has sent me flowers," Calla said kindly, moving forward to pluck the card from where it hung. *And he couldn't have done it at a more opportune time,* she tacked on mentally, smiling slightly as she read the card. Without a word she dropped the note into her purse and bent down to pick up the bouquet.

"Would you mind getting the door for me, Slade?" she murmured, sniffing the nearest bloom contentedly.

"From Chapman?" Slade asked brusquely, taking her key and fitting it into the lock. He eyed the huge bouquet as she carried it past him into the tiled hall.

"No." Deliberately Calla didn't volunteer any further information.

He followed her across the Spanish tiles into the white-walled living room. Hand-carved furniture from Mexico and some very fine Indian rugs set the gracious, south-western tone of the decor. Slade, for all his earlier interest in the place where she lived, seemed oblivious to the cool, uncluttered interior. He watched Calla set down the bouquet on the small, round pedestal table, the surface of which had been inlaid with painted tiles.

47

"So who sent the flowers, Calla?" he asked stonily, his hands thrust into the pockets of his slacks, his feet braced slightly apart. There was a grim, determined expression on the hard features and Calla smiled inwardly.

"A friend," she said quietly, stepping back to admire the bouquet. She could feel Slade behind her, and took a certain pleasure in baiting him like this.

"A male friend, I presume."

"Yes."

"Calla . . . !"

"Here, read the note, if you're so curious," she offered with apparent unconcern. He took it from her hand with a suspicious look.

"Congratulations on the coup," he read aloud, and frowned over the signature. "Gary?"

"Gary Crispin," Calla confirmed lightly. "He knew tonight represented the end of the negotiations. He's very thoughtful." Feeling on top of the situation, she smiled brilliantly. "I'd offer you some coffee, but . . ."

"Thank you," he said before she could finish, "I'll have mine black."

She blinked, undecided about how to deal with the rudeness for a moment. Then she relaxed. What did a cup of coffee matter at this point? And she was enjoying watching him stew over the source of the flowers. Without a word she moved gracefully into the yellow and green kitchen, her bronze-toned hair gleaming in the overhead light.

"Is this Crispin guy the reason you're so cool to every other male in sight?" Slade asked a little too quietly as he lounged in the doorway, arms folded across his broad chest.

She could feel his eyes on her as she went about the business of making coffee.

"Gary owns the dance studio where I take ballet lessons for exercise," she said unhelpfully.

"He's a *dancer?*" There was a note of disbelief in the gritty, rough voice.

"He used to dance with a company back east before he moved out here and opened the studio." Calla nodded, pouring hot water over instant coffee. She certainly wasn't going to go to the effort of making the drip kind. Not for this man!

"I see." There was a deliberate neutralness in his words.

Calla glanced over her shoulder and saw the unworried, totally confident look on his face.

"No." She chuckled with amused disdain. "*I* see. You're one of those typical macho types who automatically assumes all male dancers aren't all male, right?" She handed him a cup and saucer.

"Well, honey," he said soothingly, taking the coffee from her hand and meeting her eyes with laconic humor. "Everyone knows male ballet dancers are . . ."

"How fascinating," she interrupted guilelessly. "I would have thought a man of your experience would know better than to make generalizations about a group of men whose physical abilities are on a par with those of the most highly trained athlete."

Suddenly the amber gaze flamed. "Are you telling me this guy is your lover?"

At least that had driven the humor out of him, she thought in satisfaction as she walked wordlessly past him into the living room.

"Surely you don't expect me to discuss something like that with *you!*" she charged aloofly, seating herself on the dark leather couch.

"Why not?" he growled, flinging himself into the heavy wooden chair opposite and stretching out his legs. He looked like a sprawled panther, she decided. "When

49

you're mine I sure as hell expect you to make it clear to other men!"

Calla held back her temper with a supreme effort to ask politely, "If I tell you Gary Crispin is my lover will you leave me in peace?"

"No!" He glared at her. "I'd tell you to forget him."

"Then it doesn't really matter whether I admit to having an affair with him or not, does it? Either way, you're still convinced you want me?"

"You are determined to goad me this evening, aren't you?" he observed finally after a clear struggle with his own temper. He sipped coffee and watched her over the rim.

"No one's asked you to stick around and take it."

"Just call me a masochist," he told her wryly.

"There are a lot of names I'd like to call you," she said agreeably.

"Keep in mind that the first one is 'boss.' "

"Don't tell me you're going to threaten to fire me if I don't show proper respect! You made such a point of forcing me to stay on for the extra three months this evening!" she mocked.

"I knew you'd stay as soon as Lester reminded you so subtly how rough I could make things during the reorganization process," he said calmly. "Your loyalty to him and his company does you credit."

"I've already told you not to expect it to be transferred to my new employer! I will very definitely be leaving three months from tonight. And I'll be counting the days as I wait."

"I'll help you count," he said smoothly, setting down the coffee cup and getting to his feet with an easy coordination. "And we might as well start tonight!"

She realized his intention and uncurled from the couch, her manner full of the icy hauteur of a prima ballerina.

"I'd just as soon you didn't paw me any further this evening!"

He smiled dangerously, reaching out to wrap one hand around her neck with lazy menace. "Do you think you can quell me by making me feel like a clumsy boy with soiled hands? After a month of doing civilized battle with you, my sweet Calla, I'm fully prepared to engage in the uncivilized kind. And while you might be able to win an occasional skirmish during our business negotiations, you haven't got a chance in this sort of war."

"Damn you, Slade! I won't have it!"

But the grip on her neck was relentless and Calla knew instinctively she wouldn't be free until he chose to release her. Once again she decided to fall back on the passivity she had attempted earlier. To fight him would only be to stimulate him further. She had learned that lesson during the past month.

There was no anger in this kiss as there had been in the one he had forced on her at the country club. Slade bent his coffee-brown head to explore her sealed lips with deliberate thoroughness, as if he were charting new territory and putting up "No Trespassing" signs as he went.

With every ounce of her will, Calla stood stiffly in his chaining embrace, telling herself that he was every inch the same kind of man as Drew had been. Was there something about the competitive world of business that bred men like this? Arrogant, proud predators who turned into sulky little boys when their arrogance and pride was offended by a woman who refused to be controlled. Men who could handle a business threat head-on, but not a threatening woman.

"Afraid, Calla?" Slade rasped provokingly, his mouth warm and inviting as he coaxed her lips apart. "Afraid of making comparisons between me and your dancer friend?"

"There is no comparison," she whispered furiously, arching her throat to pull her mouth away from his gently marauding one. It was a mistake because he instantly began a delicate, nerve-rifling string of kisses down to the curve of her shoulder.

"I'd agree, but somehow I don't think you meant that the way I want you to mean it!"

"You're right! I have no interest in being mauled by a man who knows nothing of the civilized side of life! Who sees sex as some sort of game to be used to dominate a woman!"

She felt him grow taut under the stabbing words and realized she probably should have kept her mouth shut and let him tire of the assault in his own time.

"You don't understand!" he grated thickly, his free hand sliding up the curve of her hip to settle beneath her breast.

"No!" she cried, alarmed at the escalating sensuality in him. For the first time she began to struggle, lifting her arms to push against his chest.

Reacting to the fight in her, as she had known he would, Slade deliberately let his thumb graze the nipple he found under the black material of her gown. At the same time his grip on the back of her neck tightened steadily, drawing her closer.

"You're not nearly as cold as you'd have me believe, are you?" he rasped. He let his thumb flick back across the rising nipple and Calla couldn't hide the strange shiver that went through her.

"Slade, I don't want you touching me like this! Take your hands off me!"

"But I like touching you," he countered throatily, sliding his hands away from her breast, down and around to the base of her spine. "I want to know more about the heat

52

in you that simmers below the surface. Like a fire beneath the ocean!"

His mouth nipped lightly along her bare shoulder, tasting the skin there as if it were a new and delectable culinary delight. She felt his tongue at one point and then his teeth.

And for the first time since the disaster of her marriage, Calla knew her body, her trained and disciplined body, was reacting to a man. It was intolerable. If she was ever again to let down her guard it must not be with a man like this! She'd learned her lesson once and she was not about to let herself become blinded again!

The question of how it could be happening was beyond her at the moment. The crucial thing was to bring it all to a screeching halt.

"Let me go, Slade, or I'll scream," she said tautly, her eyes wide and full of absolute determination. "For the last time, I do not wish to be pawed by you!"

Without a word Slade lifted his head and stared down into her ice-cold eyes. She was aware of his fingers flexing at the nape of her neck as the amber in his gaze poured over her like molten gold.

"I was going to take things slowly with you," he grated hoarsely. "I was willing to give you time. I thought that I'd let you see how much I wanted you in slow doses so that you wouldn't run scared. But you, yourself, wrecked my plans by admitting you already knew how I felt. That doesn't leave me much choice, Calla. I have to leave my mark on you tonight because you've made it impossible to play the game the way I had originally intended. Can't you understand?"

"I understand you're behaving with classic male arrogance. The little boy in a man's clothes is reaching out for a new toy he feels should be his by right simply because he wants it!"

"I'm sick of your crazy psychoanalyzing," he flung back. The fingers at the back of her neck did something to the closure of the halter gown and instantly the black material of the bodice fell forward. "And you'd better stop referring to me as a boy! Don't you know that only makes me more determined than ever to teach you the difference between men and boys?"

With a startled gasp of dismay, Calla clutched at the fabric of her dress, holding it desperately in place over her small, curving breasts. Her fury leaped skyward.

"I'll never forgive you for this! You can forget about the three months I promised you tonight! I want you out of my life this minute!"

"But I'm not a tame dog you can frighten off with those ice-cold eyes and that waspish tongue!" he warned softly, too softly. His hands were wrapped around her waist now, holding her still in front of him while his eyes traveled possessively over the skin of her upper breasts and shoulders.

"Is that how you've kept the other men at bay during the past four years?" he went on with derisive humor. "Frozen them to death or terrified them until they ran off with their tails between their legs?"

"Get out of here!" she ordered, stepping back immediately as she felt his hands loosen from around her waist.

He shrugged out of his jacket and yanked at the knot of his tie, his eyes never leaving her rigid features. "I've told you," he said quietly, reaching for her once again, "I have to leave my mark on you tonight. There's too much at stake now!"

Calla slipped out of reach with the light, slightly uneven steps of a dancer. Without pausing to think she reached for a tall brass candlestick standing on the carved wooden buffet behind her. When she came around with it in one hand, still desperately clutching at her bodice with the

54

other, it was too late. Slade moved quickly, gently, simply, and devastatingly effectively. Calla lay on the floor in a soft heap, unhurt but staring up at him in amazed fury. The candlestick lay several feet away. Automatically she grabbed once again at the front of her dress but not before the tip of one high, pointed breast had been exposed to his eyes.

The sleek knot of her hair had come undone in the tussle and the light brown stuff floated around her shoulders. Too breathless for an instant to speak, she simply stared at her tormentor. Slade stood above her, his hands on his hips, the opened collar of his white shirt giving him a rakish air that was redundant. The man would have looked quite dangerous enough without it!

"I'll be the first to admit you look very sexy lying there in dishabille," he said dryly, "but I honestly hadn't planned on using judo to catch my future wife!"

"Your wife!" Calla could only stare at him speechlessly, wondering if he had gone crazy or if she had.

"Don't look so startled, sweetheart," he said in a gentling voice as he crouched down beside her and touched her cheek in a caressing motion that made her flinch. "On the other hand, that startled look is at least a change from the waves of the North Atlantic that have been lapping me all evening."

"Slade, will you stop making fun of me?" she bit out, levering herself to a sitting position and attempting to refasten the halter of her dress with shaking fingers. "I realize you must find this all very humorous, but I . . . oh!"

He reached out and grabbed her hands before she could complete the small task, and then he yanked her lightly across his lap as he settled down onto the carpet.

"I'm not finding this in the least amusing," he assured her, the mocking look turning to one of growing passion as he moved the flat of his hand down her throat and across her breast, dragging the black material down to her waist. "I hadn't meant to propose like this at all. You are ruining every one of my fine plans!"

He lowered his head to seal the protest behind her lips, his palm gliding between the shallow valley of her breasts. His tongue pierced the darkness of her mouth as his fingers began tracing delicate patterns around a nipple.

"Don't be afraid of me," he whispered huskily against her lips as he held her cradled in his lap. "I won't hurt you . . ."

"Let me go!" she said with a soft cry of rage and despair. She couldn't move. He was holding her gently but firmly, leaving her tense body no room to maneuver. Her head lay against his thigh and she could feel the muscled strength of it.

"No," he soothed, his fingers coaxing and tantalizing on her breast before they began a light filigree pattern down to her stomach. "I didn't hurt you a minute ago. I know exactly how much force I applied and I didn't let you take a hard fall."

"Please, Slade . . ."

"God! You have a fine, strong body, little one. I can feel the strength in you beneath my fingers. Is that from your dancing? Who would have thought dancing could give a body power and grace?" he added whimsically, his lips scorching along her throat. "Perhaps you were born with it!"

"Slade, I won't let you seduce me!" she vowed, her voice a thread of sound, but nonetheless laced with her determined will. Why did it have to be this man who broke through all the carefully erected barriers? Why did it have to be Slade York who could bring her body to life?

"You can't stop me, sweetheart," he muttered, his tongue curling around a nipple as his hand probed along the lacy edge of her briefs. "I want you too badly. And a man has a right to seduce the woman he's going to marry," he concluded with absolute conviction.

"No man has any rights over a woman except those she chooses to grant!"

But even as she voiced her defiance, her fingers, which had been trapped against his lower chest, trembled as they moved fitfully and encountered the warm skin of him where one of his buttons had come undone. She tried to pull them away as if she had touched a live flame.

"I guess I'm old-fashioned then," he chuckled huskily, closing his teeth with incredible gentleness around the aroused tip of her breast. "I believe in things like husbandly rights and privileges!"

"Will you stop talking that nonsense!" she rasped, aware of an unfamiliar twinge in her loins. A twinge that, although it was very mild, immediately sent shock waves through her system. No! It wasn't possible! Not even with Drew had she known the ultimate plateau in lovemaking. She told herself that her senses deceived her; that she couldn't recognize the first stirrings of an impending sensation she had never experienced in her husband's arms! How could her body recognize what it had never known?

"It's not nonsense," Slade gritted as he moved his head down toward her navel, trailing biting little kisses in a path of fire. The path culminated when his tongue dipped into the sensitive depression in her stomach. "I'm going to make you mine, Calla Nevin. Completely mine!"

"No!" It was a protest compounded of feminine fear and angry rejection. But in that moment Calla couldn't honestly have said what it was she was rejecting. It could have been Slade's sensuous attack on her body or it could have been her reaction to the assault.

He didn't bother to argue against her denial. Instead he shifted both his weight and her own, settling her flat onto the carpet and stretching himself alongside until he partially covered her body.

"Can you even imagine how I've longed to see you like this?" he demanded with rough savagery as his hand spread out across her vulnerable stomach. "I've wanted you from the first day we met. I took one look at those beautiful eyes, saw the way you moved as you came forward to greet me, and I knew!"

Calla met the heated amber gaze and tried to struggle back from the edge of the yawning pit that stretched before her. Summoning all the discipline, both mental and physical, for which she had fought so hard during the past four years, she refused to give way before the dominant maleness in him.

"You knew what, Slade? That you'd found another woman to add to your string of conquests?" she asked steadily.

He put his hand over her mouth, his eyes meeting hers over the edge of his palm. "I've told you, I'm going to marry you, woman! Will you stop talking about conquests?"

"I doubt if I'll ever marry again, Slade York," she managed when he allowed her to speak. "But if I decide to risk it again it sure as hell won't be with a man who has no idea of how to go about creating an enduring relationship! Never again will I tie myself to a man who has to dominate a woman in order to prove his own masculinity to himself! A man who is incapable of accepting a woman as an equal because to do so threatens his ego. And most of all I wouldn't choose a man who shows all the hallmarks of the kind of male, who, when he fails to dominate his own woman, turns to another!"

He stared at her with a suddenly unreadable expression. "So that's it," he finally observed slowly. "He couldn't handle you so he went off to find a woman he could handle."

"Several of them!" she acknowledged forcefully, not pretending to misunderstand his reference to her ex-husband. "Just as you seem to have done since you left your wife!"

For a moment she thought she'd gone too far. She felt him tense, as if he were coiled to retaliate with physical punishment and regardless of her resolve, Calla shivered. In spite of her dancer's strength, there was no denying that he was far more powerful than she and if he chose to use that power against her . . .

"You know nothing about my divorce or the women I've had since my marriage ended," he gritted between clenched teeth. "You better learn not to jump to conclusions!"

"And what if I don't?" she taunted rashly, her temper flaring anew at his arrogance. It was typical of a man like this to resort to intimidation first. Perhaps when he realized she wouldn't bow to it, he would leave in disgust.

"You will!" he admitted fiercely. "It's damn obvious you pulled yourself out of that mess of a marriage by your bootstraps and I'd be a fool if I didn't recognize the strength in you now to do whatever is demanded of you."

"Then you ought to be making your exit, because I'm going to use every bit of that strength against you!" she flung back desperately.

"Be my guest," he invited with a totally unexpected smile as he got lithely to his feet and pulled her up beside him. "You won't turn me into a sulky little boy by trying to prove yourself my equal."

Calla ground her teeth as he took the ends of the dress and fastened them gently behind her neck. Trembling with reaction and anger, she stood still as he finished the task and then dropped a light kiss on her nape—a very proprietary kiss that made her long to slap him.

"You really managed to throw everything into a tailspin tonight, didn't you?" he whispered wistfully as his hands came back down on her bare shoulders and he tugged her back against his body. He bent to breathe in the scent of her loosened hair.

"I did nothing except let you know I was aware of your arrogant plans!"

"But you didn't know all of my plans, did you?" he teased, nibbling at the tip of her ear as he pulled the hair on one side of her head back behind it. "You didn't know I meant to marry you, did you?"

"What difference does it make? I'm no more interested in marriage with you than I am in an affair!"

"Tell me that three months from now." She could sense his laughing smile.

"If you think I'm going to work for you . . . !" she began seethingly.

"You will," he said confidently. "You've got all those inefficient, redundant people on Lester's old staff to protect, remember?"

"You wouldn't dare let people go!" she gasped as he stepped away from her and went to retrieve his jacket. "You issued a statement saying you wouldn't terminate anyone for the first year!" She whirled to face him, knowing he wouldn't hesitate to make good on his threat even as she denied the possibility.

"I issued a statement to that effect, yes. But it wasn't written into the contract!"

He pulled on the jacket, feeling automatically for the case in his pocket, and smiled down into her enraged eyes. "Good night, sweetheart," he murmured politely as he kissed her forehead and headed for the door.

He paused, his hand on the knob, to glance back over

his shoulder at the bouquet on the little table. "By the way, tell your friend, what's-his-name, that I don't want to find his flowers on the doorstep again! Regardless of the status of his masculinity!"

An instant later he was gone into the warm Arizona night.

CHAPTER FOUR

Calla came down from the series of entrechats, alighting in fifth position with the left foot in front, and knew even as she dragged air into her lungs that Miss Marsden was not going to be pleased.

"No, no, no! What is the matter with you today, Calla?" the older woman snapped unpleasantly as she ignored the other adult pupils to concentrate on Calla's failures. "You have been taking lessons long enough to know that the knees must be straight while in midair. Try it again!"

The tiny, imperious little woman known only as Miss Marsden clapped her hands to signal the required beats of the legs as Calla obediently sank slightly in a plié, jumped, crossed the right leg in a straight-legged beat, and once again descended in fifth with the left foot in front.

"Better, better! Let us try a series of them now!" Miss Marsden's snapping black eyes brooked no excuses, especially not the ridiculous one of exhaustion. Her head, with its graying black hair drawn into a proper ballet style bun, bobbed in time as she again clapped her hands for the required jumps and leg beats.

"Enough!" she exclaimed finally, turning back to the rest of the class. "You will do better at this when you come for your evening lesson next week, yes?"

"Yes, ma'am," Calla agreed submissively, trying to get her breath without being obvious about it. Her legs were trembling from the physical effort and she stole a look at the clock. Another fifteen minutes left in the lesson. Fifteen minutes under Miss Marsden could be a very long time.

Eventually, to Calla's vast relief, the group of twelve

women in black tights and leotards moved together in the traditional ending of the lesson, the classical bow to Miss Marsden. She clapped her hands once more and the women, for the first time in an hour and a half, were allowed to relax.

"Good grief! Miss Marsden certainly was on your case this morning." Angie Connors grinned as the two women walked side by side to the dressing area and began removing their soft black leather slippers. All of the dancing clothes were of a uniform color. Black. Miss Marsden did not encourage creativity in the uniform. All creativity must be channeled into the dance.

"I got to bed late last night," Calla admitted ruefully, stuffing her shoes into her bag and reaching for a pair of jeans to pull on over her tights and leotard. She was soaking wet with perspiration but she decided to save the shower until she got home. A glance in the mirror showed the knot of her hair was still in place, but other than that she looked as if she'd been through the proverbial wringer.

"What sort of excuse is that!" Angie exclaimed in Marsden accents. "A dancer's first duty is to her body!"

"Only so that she won't disgrace herself when she is dancing," Calla concluded with a wry chuckle. "I don't think Miss Marsden cares about our bodies, only about the dance itself. As if it were something tangible that must be treated with utmost respect!"

"Which is precisely the case!" said a laughing male voice as the two women emerged from the dressing room. A man stood waiting out in the hall, his Byronic dark eyes and black hair giving him a theatrical look that he wore very well. His body was the compact, well-developed one of the professional male dancer although he was approaching forty.

"Gary!" Calla admonished with a grin as Angie smiled

and waved good-bye. "No fair listening in on students' comments!"

"The dancing master sees all and knows all," he intoned dramatically.

"Including my home address," she concluded, nodding. "I got the flowers. They were lovely, Gary. Thanks!"

He watched her run a small terry towel around her exposed neck and shoulders. "I'm glad you liked them. How did the celebration go at the country club?"

"Very well," Calla affirmed noncommittally. "Perhaps a little too well. I had trouble maintaining Miss Marsden's standards of concentration this morning!" she added with a grimace.

"She is a taskmaster, isn't she?" He smiled in satisfaction. "I was lucky to get her for an instructor."

"Does she handle the little kids the same way she handles the adults?"

"Oh, yes. Absolute and unswerving concentration and discipline," he said seriously. "Miss Marsden's goal is perfection!"

Calla smiled. "It's nice of you to give your adult exercise class the benefit of one of your best instructors, Gary. She conducts a lesson as if we really were potential ballerinas instead of a bunch of career women trying to stay in shape!"

He shrugged. "The ballet has something to teach everyone. Why should I withhold the best from any of my students? But you're dripping wet. You should get into a shower," he went on, frowning emphatically.

"Exactly where I'm headed." Calla stepped forward quickly and put a hand briefly on his arm. "Thanks again for the flowers, Gary. It was very thoughtful of you."

"I knew you were expending a great deal of energy on those negotiations," he said gently. "Miss Marsden's been yelling at you for nearly a month so I figured a lot of your

65

strength wasn't going into the dance. I assume that will change now, hmm?"

"You sound like a quieter version of Miss Marsden!" she scolded. "Whatever adversely affects the dancing must be gotten out of the way!"

"I'm glad you understand. We'll make a dancer out of you yet!"

Calla laughed and dug her keys out of her leather bag as she headed for the door. She felt much better, she decided with a measure of satisfaction, as she started the engine of her bright green Fiat. She might not have pleased Miss Marsden this morning but Miss Marsden's insistence on concentration and physical control had done a great deal for Calla's chaotic frame of mind.

The discipline of the ballet gave Calla the renewed feeling of being able to deal with herself and with Slade York. She had been in a weakened condition last night, she decided as she drove toward home in the rising heat of the morning sun, weakened from a month of doing battle with him on an intellectual level. It was perhaps not surprising she had been unprepared to meet his challenge on a physical plane.

But this morning she felt back in control of her body and her mind. Lester Chapman had been right last night when he had warned her obliquely about the dangers of not supervising the transition period during York's reorganization of the firm. Someone needed to cushion the impact and who better than Calla? She certainly knew him better than anyone else after the past month!

It wouldn't be a pleasant three months, she thought grimly as she turned down her street. But if she kept her head she could survive. The crucial thing was to keep out of York's physical reach. She must not find herself in the position she had wound up in last night. The man was potentially dangerous. Every instinct warned her of that.

She was frowning as she tried to force the memories of the previous evening out of her head, thinking of ways in which Slade York could be handled, and she didn't really notice the silver Mercedes until she had parked her own car in the lot.

When she did notice it, Calla experienced an undeniable moment of pure panic in spite of her renewed determination to remain in charge of herself and the situation. Was the man going to hound her every step?

Angrily she gripped the strap of her leather shoulder bag and paced deliberately toward the door of her condominium.

He was sitting on the doorstep, reading the Saturday paper, a plastic cup of coffee from a nearby fast-food restaurant by his side. He didn't see her at first and Calla had a second's impression of the rich coffee shade of his hair in the morning sunlight as he bent over the headlines. He was wearing the dark-framed glasses, which somehow gave the rugged features an almost intellectual air. His jeans were snug and faded and the blue workshirt also looked as if it had been through a number of washings. The shirt was open at the collar and rolled up on his forearms. Calla forced her eyes away from the sprinkling of dark hair on his tanned, sinewy arm.

"No offense," she muttered mockingly as she came to a halt in front of him, "but I'd rather come home to flowers on my doorstep than you!"

He lifted his head slowly, his amber gaze moving from the toes of her sandal-shod feet, up the length of her legs, and coming to rest for an instant on the expanse of skin exposed by the scooped neckline of the leotard.

"I'm sure you didn't mean any offense," Slade said quite gently as he absently removed his glasses and stuffed them into the leather case, "but I'm offended nevertheless." His eyes, unshielded by the lenses of his glasses now, moved

67

on up to her set face. "I come in peace," he intoned, a slow smile curving his mouth.

"Do you even know the meaning of the word?" she sighed, stepping around him to open her door.

"Calla," he said, getting to his feet and picking up the half-empty coffee cup. "I have to talk to you. . . ."

"I'll be in my office Tuesday morning," she informed him regally, turning to shut the door in his face. It wouldn't close. Probably because of the large foot he had thrust over the threshold, she decided with an inner groan.

"Calla, please, honey," he said with soft intent, his eyes meeting hers through the small opening of the door. "Just listen to me for a few minutes, will you? I'm sorry about last night. . . ."

That startled her but she made an effort not to show it. "Sorry?" she blazed tightly. "Sorry you didn't get what you wanted?"

He drew a long breath, clearly trying to stay reasonable. "Will you please hear me out?"

"I can't right now. I've got to take a shower."

"I'll wait."

"Not in my house, you won't!"

"You're in a charming frame of mind, aren't you? Are you always like this when you come from your ballet class?"

"Aha! I detect a lessening of your peaceful intentions," she pounced sweetly. "Losing our temper already, are we?"

"No, damn it! I'm not going to lose my temper!"

"Don't look now, but I think you already have."

He visibly restrained his next comment and gently but forcefully began to push against the door she was attempting to shut in his face. "We have to talk, Calla. Go ahead and take your shower. I'll wait for you in the living room."

He cocked a brow questioningly. "Unless you're going to resort to screaming for assistance from the neighbors?"

"If I did would you retreat?"

"No."

She believed him. But he didn't really look all that menacing this morning, she decided. Merely determined. Could it be he truly was sorry for the scene the previous evening? She eyed him skeptically and let the door swing open.

"I'll be out in a few minutes," she told him quellingly, disappearing down the hall in the direction of her bedroom.

She didn't deliberately rush the shower, but somehow Calla, who loved to linger in the hot water, found herself toweling briskly after only a few minutes. She redid her hair into the habitual sleek knot, pulled on jeans and a short-sleeved plaid shirt, and slipped back into her sandals. The physical exhaustion was gone, replaced by the marvelously invigorated sensation a session of dance always left. She was ready to take on the world again.

"How did you know I'd be returning this morning?" she asked coolly as she reentered the living room and found him leafing through a large coffee-table book on ballet. Once again he removed his glasses and stored them.

"Your neighbor said you always had a dance class on Saturday mornings," he said without any expression, watching as she walked past him into the kitchen and started to make a cup of tea for herself.

Something in the very lack of intonation alerted Calla. She stooped slightly to peer at him through the opening of the breakfast bar.

"You asked my neighbor where I was?" she questioned forbiddingly.

"I, uh, couldn't imagine where you could have disappeared to so early on a Saturday morning," he admitted placatingly, his eyes curiously enigmatic.

Calla straightened at the whistle of the tea kettle and turned back to her small preparations. "Where did you think I was?"

There was silence from the other room.

"Slade?" she pressed in open annoyance. She picked up her cup and saucer and walked back to the living room.

"Don't look at me like that," he pleaded wryly. "I'll admit I was a little upset at the various possibilities, but I swear I didn't make any sort of scene with your neighbor. . . ."

"I should hope not!" Calla grated feelingly. She saw his amber gaze flick narrowingly at the bouquet of flowers, which still stood on the little table, and knew exactly what had worried him.

"If I had spent the night somewhere else after you left," she told him cuttingly, "it wouldn't be any of your business."

"How can you say that when I've told you we're going to be married?" he protested softly.

Calla wasn't at all certain she liked this new, reproachful Slade. She didn't trust his seeming determination to avoid an out-and-out slinging match.

"I can say it because I have no intention of marrying you," she retorted simply. "Now, why don't you tell me what it is that brought you over here so bright and early this morning. The sooner you're on your way, the sooner I can do my washing."

He looked positively hurt. "Do you have any idea what it does to a man's ego to be told he's not as interesting as doing the weekly wash?"

"If I thought a listing of all the things I'd rather be doing than talking to you would put a serious dent in your ego, I'd start rattling them off," she assured him, taking a defiant sip of tea.

The amber gaze narrowed slightly as he watched her hair turn briefly to bronze in the light of the morning sun streaming in through the sliding glass doors that led out onto the patio.

"Calla," he began determinedly, "I'm sorry about last night."

She looked up and her sea-colored eyes clashed with his. "Sorry you asked me to marry you or sorry you forced your attentions on me or sorry you blackmailed me into working for you?"

His mouth twisted wryly. "I seem to have a lot for which to apologize."

"I'll agree with that."

"Would you do me the honor of accepting my apology?" he asked carefully.

"When you tell me exactly why you're apologizing."

Humor filtered into the amber gaze and Calla saw the crinkly lines at the corners of his eyes deepen slightly. He was repressing a smile.

"I should know by now you're a very cautious negotiator," he observed.

"I've had a lot of experience during the past month," she reminded him pointedly.

He inhaled slowly, meditatively. "I want us to start from scratch, Calla. I want to be allowed to, well, court you. What I'm apologizing for is having allowed matters to get out of hand last night. I never meant to rush you, little one. I knew you were the sort of woman who needed some time. But somehow, after you admitted you'd known all along how much I want you, everything seemed to escalate at once. And I'd already waited so long to kiss you . . ."

"This doesn't sound like much of an apology to me!"

71

Calla gritted, secretly appalled by this new approach. What was he up to now?

"But it is," he insisted, getting restlessly to his feet and walking toward the sliding glass doors. He shoved his hands into the back pocket of his jeans and stared moodily out onto the patio.

"I'm accepting the blame for letting my emotions run ahead of my common sense. How much more of an apology can you expect from a man?"

"It strikes me you don't know the first thing about apologizing," Calla announced, desperately trying to sort out the underlying possibilities of the situation. She stared at his broad back and thought furiously.

"I'm doing my best," he told her quietly. "Will you please accept that I'm sorry for having rushed you last night . . ."

"For having forced yourself on me?"

"Yes, dammit!"

"I don't believe you."

"All right!" He swung around to glare at her. "I'm not sorry I kissed you, touched you. God knows I've wanted to do it often enough during the past few weeks! But I won't push you again beyond the limits you're willing to go! Please believe me!"

There was a charged tension in the silent room as Calla studied his golden eyes. He looked annoyed but he also looked quite determined. If he really meant it . . .

"You give me your word?" Her chin lifted royally as if she were a queen grilling a subject. Her mind was still pulling apart the various uses of the situation.

"I give you my word! If you'll agree to let me court you for the next three months," he amended after the smallest of pauses.

"Are we negotiating again, Slade?"

He bit back what she knew would have been a rather

72

vicious remark and said simply, "I suppose so. And I freely admit you seem to have the upper hand."

Three months was a long time to put up with a man who made life as uncomfortable as Slade had made life last night, Calla reflected. But three months of him *courting* her instead of laying siege to her might be tolerable. It might give her a certain amount of control over him that could be extremely valuable.

She had absolutely no intention of ultimately marrying the man, naturally, but if he thought she was willing to consider the idea, he might be far more manageable. Calla swallowed in the face of her own audacity.

"No more fancy judo throws?" she murmured tentatively.

He grimaced. "I should never have let things get to the point where you felt obliged to grab a weapon," he stated flatly. "It won't happen again."

She considered that. "Where did you learn judo, anyhow?"

He blinked at the unexpected question. "Is it important?"

"No. I was merely curious."

"Maybe that's a good sign. You've never shown much curiosity about me before! The answer to your question is that I was introduced to it in college."

"I see."

"Calla?"

"I'm thinking about it, Slade." She took another sip of tea, but her mind was made up. She would accept his offer to reduce the intensity of his pursuit. It would give her the breathing room she needed for the next three months.

Finally she set the cup and saucer down onto the heavy wooden table in front of the couch and said witheringly, "You will behave yourself? There won't be any repeat performances on a par with last night's?"

"I won't push you," he agreed. "As long as you uphold your end of the deal."

"What, exactly, does that imply?"

"That you'll accept my invitations and allow me the chance to woo you properly," he explained unhesitatingly.

"And you won't drag our personal affairs into work?"

"No."

She gave a crisp, affirmative nod. "All right. I'm willing to give it a try."

She saw the tension seep out of him and the satisfied demeanor that replaced it. Calla watched him suspiciously, but he only said politely, "Thank you. And now I'd like to issue my first invitation."

She bit her lip unconsciously, not at all sure she had done the right thing. But what choice did she have? If she was going to work for him for the next three months surely it would be better to exert some control rather than none at all over his actions.

"I've got a lot of things to do this afternoon, Slade," she began repressively.

"I know. The wash. But I've got something much more interesting to suggest," he offered with a grin. "Have you ever been soaring?"

"Soaring! Well, no, I haven't. I only fly when it's absolutely necessary!"

"Powered flight isn't the same thing at all. That's a means of transportation," he said, waving a dismissing hand. "Soaring is the closest thing to having your own set of wings. Come with me, Calla, and I'll show you what it's like to really fly."

"Is it safe?"

"Today we won't even be out of sight of the airport, and the weather is terrific. Did you see all those nice puffy cumulus clouds starting to form above the desert floor this morning? Lots of nice thermals. Please, Calla?" He held out both hands innocently. "I won't be able to assault you while I'm handling the controls, you know!"

Well, why not, Calla thought. It would give him the impression she was serious about letting him have a chance to carry out his "courtship." It would establish the notion that she had negotiated in good faith. Would she be able to keep him thinking that for the full three months? Or would this little scheme collapse when he realized she was stringing him along? There were a lot of adjectives Calla could have used to describe Slade York, but stupid wasn't one of them.

"Let me dump this cup in the sink," she finally said, capitulating reluctantly.

"Don't rush. There's a little matter I want to take care of while you're rinsing out the cup."

She nodded as she walked back into the kitchen. She was aware of the sliding glass door opening as she ran water into the sink. Slade must have taken a shortcut out to his car. Calla set the cup and saucer on the drainboard to dry and looked around automatically to make certain the stove was turned off.

When she walked back into the living room, he still hadn't returned. She glanced around absently, aware of something slightly different. And then she realized the vase of Gary's flowers and its contents were gone.

When Slade reappeared, crossing the patio and stepping through the open window, she was waiting for him.

"What have you done with my flowers!" she snapped, glaring at the way he was dusting off one hand against the other.

He looked back at her blandly. "They were starting to wilt. Nothing worse than dying flowers, you know. Very depressing."

"The hell they were! They were fresh last night and this morning! Slade York, I won't have you interfering in my private life just because I've agreed to let you try your courting technique on me! Do you understand?"

"Let's go, honey, I don't want to miss the good flying weather!"

"But my flowers . . . !"

"It's too late," he assured her kindly, taking her resisting arm and leading her swiftly out the front door. "Even if you could retrieve them from the garbage, you wouldn't want them now. Your neighbor had pizza last night. The flowers landed on top of the leftovers!"

"Of all the nerve! If this is any sample of your new, improved approach, let me tell you, I don't . . ."

The rest of her words were cut off as she found herself pushed lightly onto the Mercedes seat and the door shut in her face. In the short span of time it took Slade to lope easily around the front of the car and open his own door, Calla knew her sense of humor was rising to meet the situation.

The thought of laughing at his antics was unnerving, to say the least, but Calla barely managed to restrain the grin that tugged at her lips.

"If you want flowers, I'll buy you some more," he promised lightly, slanting a glance at her profile.

"The first thing you're going to have to learn about 'courting' me, Slade, is that I'm not fond of jealous, possessive men. Neither emotion indicates a great love so don't try telling me any different. Jealousy and possessiveness are only signs of . . ."

"Please don't call me a little boy again," he interrupted quietly, his tone at that suspiciously neutral stage once more. Out of the corner of her eye Calla saw his fingers tighten on the wheel.

Unaccountably, she decided to back off from her goading remark. Whether she did so out of fear or because she suddenly found herself not wanting to ruin the afternoon

76

with an argument, she couldn't have said. Neither reason was very satisfactory and she worried about it all the way to the airport.

"It looks like a toy!" Calla exclaimed sometime later as she stood eyeing askance the sleek little sailplane as it rested on the tip of one aluminum wing. A single wheel under the belly appeared to be the only concession the designers had made toward providing landing gear.

Slade grinned proudly as he flipped open the clear cockpit cover, exposing seats arranged in tandem. "Don't worry, it flies like a bird."

"It's about the size of one," Calla remarked as she lowered herself precariously down into the rear seat. "Are you sure I won't put a foot through the hull? It's like getting into a canoe for the first time!"

"If you do, you better believe I'll send you the bill. This sailplane is my most valued possession. Outside of you, that is," he added with a wicked grin that Calla thought it best to ignore. "Here, buckle the shoulder harness."

He leaned inside the cockpit to adjust it for her. Once again Calla kept her mouth shut, refraining from pointing out that she knew how to deal with seat belts.

She glanced apprehensively around the runway, where the little plane sat waiting patiently. Ahead of them a Cessna 180, looking much more like a vehicle designed for flying, stood waiting for the signal.

"Is that towrope the only thing that guarantees we get airborne?" Calla demanded, glaring at the cord that connected the Cessna and the sailplane.

"For someone with a background in technology, you're not displaying much faith in the wonders of aeronautical theory," Slade complained, climbing into the front seat and buckling his own harness. He shut the cockpit, waved to the Cessna's pilot, then nodded to a gangling young man who had detached himself from one of the nearby hangars. Immediately their assistant lifted the wingtip off the ground.

"Airplanes ought to have engines," Calla declared stoutly as the Cessna roared to life and began moving down the runway.

The towrope tautened and the little sailplane began moving in the wake of the towplane. The helpful young man ran alongside, holding the wingtip until there was enough speed to maintain balance.

It seemed only a few seconds before the Cessna was off the ground and Calla's fingers curled into the seat as the sailplane followed, becoming airborne with astonishing ease. At once the little toy of a vehicle seemed sure of itself. She could only hope it would continue to feel that way when the Cessna left them behind.

"How high before we get abandoned to our fate?" she demanded, leaning forward to talk to Slade. The sound of the Cessna's single engine provided a pleasant illusion of powered flight.

"About three thousand feet or so," Slade said, his eyes on his instruments.

"Are those York instruments?" she asked, following his glance.

"The airspeed indicator and the rate-of-climb indicator are," he confirmed with a nod.

The Cessna made wide, lazy circles, drawing the sailplane higher and higher above the desert floor. Below them Calla saw the city, relatively flat in design except for the scattering of high rises reflecting its cosmopolitan, eastern influence. The mountains that guarded Phoenix and the Salt River Valley took on a new perspective.

Calla was just beginning to enjoy the view when Slade reached for the red knob in front of him. A second later the sailplane was on its own, the released towrope trailing behind the Cessna, which turned back toward the airport.

CHAPTER FIVE

"Oh, my goodness," Calla said in a very small voice, realizing just how soothing the drone of an engine was when one was several thousand feet in the air. Slowly she became aware of another sound, the hiss of air as the sailplane slipped through its natural element. Was this what it sounded like to a bird?

"How are you doing back there?" Slade demanded lightly from the front seat. She knew he was enjoying himself enormously.

"I'm adjusting, I think," she retorted dryly. "At least we didn't fall right down out of the sky the minute you released the rope. I was half expecting that, you know."

"Like I said, no faith in the theory of flight," he chuckled. "Do you think a bird worries about falling out of the sky?"

"A bird has wings that flap," she pointed out.

"He doesn't exert himself when he can get a free ride on the air currents! Haven't you ever watched a hawk climbing in circles without moving his wings? A natural-born glider pilot!"

"I'll have to admit, it's a different sensation altogether than powered flight. Much more . . . free, I guess."

"Like the difference between swimming with a swimsuit and without one," he laughed.

"Slade!"

"Watch this, we're going to chase some thermals."

Calla was aware they had been moving upward in a tight spiral, riding a rising bubble of air that had been under them since the towplane had been left behind. When

Slade banked, heading away from the cushioning thrust of air, there was a faint sinking sensation.

The sailplane quickly found another thermal and once again Slade turned into it in crisp, close spirals. They climbed another thousand feet in height. Calla began to relax. She caught occasional glimpses of the airport below and felt reassured. She knew enough about flying to know that even powered aircraft could glide safely back to an airport without an engine if they had enough altitude.

"I can't get over how quiet it is," she said in faint awe. "Only the rush of air."

"I know. It's fantastic, isn't it?" Slade's voice held pleased satisfaction.

"How do you know where the thermals are going to be?" Calla asked as they seemed to lose the upward thrust of air they had been riding and Slade went off in search of another.

"You don't. At least, not for certain. But there are a lot of clues. That little cloud over there may be forming because of one, for example."

Slade guided the little sailplane toward the marshmallow and sure enough when they were underneath the small craft rose eagerly. At the base of the cloud, Slade banked away again.

"And often a road surface will be hotter than the surrounding desert. The air above it will rise because it's warmed more than the neighboring air."

Once again he proved his point, gliding over a two-lane road far below and being rewarded with more altitude.

"You look for contrasts in the terrain where the sun might have caused uneven heating of the surface. Where there's uneven heating and cooling there's a chance a bubble of the warmer air will be released. You know the laws of thermodynamics, I trust?"

"I'm aware that warmer air rises," she muttered with a touch of resentment.

"Good girl. Okay, it's all yours."

"What!" Calla's momentary resentment faded in the face of the shock. "Slade! Don't tease me like this! Put your hands back on that stick, for heaven's sake!"

"Why should I? You've got one in front of you, too!"

"I don't know what I'm doing! Are you out of your mind?"

The sailplane began to act a little sloppy and Calla realized Slade was probably better at playing "chicken" than she was. Hastily she closed her fingers around the control. An experimental movement brought instant response from the sailplane.

Encouraged and with a sense of excitement, she tried it again. Soon she was guiding the obedient, aluminum-skinned bird into a rising spiral.

"My God! One could get addicted to this kind of power!" She laughed as her confidence grew.

"I'm aware of that," Slade said on a dry chuckle.

"You know, in spite of your bossiness and general arrogance, I'll bet you don't lack for dates on Saturday mornings!"

There was a silence from the front seat and then Slade said quite calmly, "You're the first woman I've ever taken soaring with me."

"Oh."

Calla didn't know what else to say to that so she concentrated very hard on her first gliding lesson.

For another hour they chased thermals, soaring and banking and climbing with the freedom of a bird. By the time Slade took the controls for the last time and started the sailplane in a gentle, shallow glide back toward the airport, Calla was willing to forget the incident of the garbaged flowers entirely.

"What if an airplane is also coming in to land?" she asked as Slade lined up the nose of the craft with the runway below.

"We have the right of way," he assured her. "Powered craft give way to unpowered ones. And this is known as a soaring field so other pilots are on the lookout for us."

A few moments later the sailplane touched down lightly on its single wheel and rolled lightly along the runway. Using the ailerons, Slade kept the wings level until the vehicle came to a complete halt on the side of the pavement. Two young men standing near a hangar hurried forward to help drag the sailplane back home by its tail.

Slade supervised the storing of his pride and joy and then hooked an arm around Calla's shoulders to guide her back to the Mercedes. When she made an instinctive movement to slip away he ignored it, hauling her almost imperceptibly closer. And, somehow, perhaps because he looked so pleased with himself and with life at that moment, she couldn't find the inner ruthlessness it would have taken to resist his light hold.

"I knew you'd like soaring," he told her on a note of satisfaction as he opened the car door. "You took to it like a natural. We'll do it again next weekend!"

Calla turned genuinely regretful eyes on him as he slid behind the wheel. "Thank you, Slade. I'd love to, but I can't. I've got other plans for next weekend."

"The whole weekend?" he growled, his amber eyes hardening abruptly as he paused, key in hand, to stare at her.

"I'm afraid so. Business." For the life of her she didn't know why she was bothering to apologize!

"Business! What business? You work for York Instruments now. I don't know of any reason you can't be free next weekend!"

"Slade, I'm going to a conference down in Tucson. It's

82

been planned for months. Lester always sends someone and this year it's my turn."

"That two-day meeting on state-of-the-art instrumentation?" he clarified with a narrowed gaze.

"That's right."

He relaxed and turned the key in the ignition. "That's no problem. I've already got people from the company scheduled to go. York Instruments will be well-represented without you."

"I'm planning to go as much for my own sake as for the company's," Calla stated evenly, not looking at him as he backed the Mercedes out of the parking lot and headed it for the highway toward town. "The reservations have all been made and I'm looking forward to it. It's an important conference here in the Southwest."

She felt him assimilating the firmness in her voice and knew he was searching for a logical way around her arguments. She also knew instinctively that he didn't want to be logical about it. He wanted to be able to tell her she couldn't go and have that be the end of the matter. Of course, if it were a conference *he* wanted to attend, he wouldn't think of letting a woman talk him out of it!

"What if I said York Instruments isn't going to pay your way? That we already have enough money committed to the trip and don't intend to send any more people?" The slightly gritty voice held that suspiciously neutral tone again.

Deliberately Calla forced an uncaring shrug. "I'll pay my own way if that's the company's feeling on the matter. I've been looking forward to the conference for weeks. There are several seminars scheduled that are going to be extremely useful to me."

"We'll talk about it later," Slade told her, causing Calla to glance sideways at him in deep suspicion. But the hard lines of his face were bland and clueless.

"There's nothing more to discuss," she said coolly.

"Yes, there is, but we'll do it over dinner. Where would you like to eat this evening?"

Calla drew a deep breath and then astonished herself by saying lightly, "You don't seem very concerned about my washing!"

"You can do it this afternoon. I'll pick you up at six, and since you don't seem to have any preferences I'll take you to a place I know over in Scottsdale. Great Mexican food and lots of atmosphere!"

Two hours later, as Calla put through her last load of wash, she was still asking herself how she'd come to find herself saddled with a dinner date in the company of Slade York. It was the soaring experience that had weakened her, she decided grimly, stuffing her towels into the washer. It had created a sense of euphoria in both of them and he'd taken advantage of the temporary weakness. She slammed the washer lid shut and stalked back into the kitchen.

Well, she was committed to the evening, and if she stuck by her earlier decision to let Slade think he was courting her, she was probably committed to several more evenings. How long before he realized she had no intention of being wooed and won? That she was only using him as he had planned to use her?

And how good a plan was it, after all? she wondered later as she began to dress for dinner. Slade was a born manager, accustomed to maneuvering people and business situations. He wasn't the type to let himself be managed in turn. Which was exactly what Calla was proposing to do.

If only she didn't feel obliged to stay around during the next three months, she thought with a groan as she slipped the starkly patterned turquoise and white dress over her

84

head. It fell to her knees in soft folds, outlining her narrow waist, and it provided a scooped neckline to emphasize the elegant line of her throat.

With a frown of concentration, Calla added a turquoise and silver necklace and then brushed her hair into a shining knot at the nape of her neck.

The admiration in Slade's eyes when she opened the door to him fifteen minutes later took her by surprise. It had been so long since she had found herself watching for a hint of masculine approval. The realization shook her and she tried a tentative withdrawal in her attitude. A withdrawal that grew more pronounced when he leaned forward to brush her lips with a short, hard little kiss.

"You look lovely tonight, little Calla. But, then, you always seem to look special. Even in those prim business suits you wear to the office!"

"I hadn't realized you didn't approve of my office attire," she remarked aloofly as she pulled away from his kiss. He looked very good himself, tonight. A fact of which he was probably aware, she thought wryly. His conservative yet casual style in clothes suited him perfectly. Dressed in dark, close-fitting slacks, a pale yellow shirt, and a chocolate brown jacket, he was the image of the coolly confident executive, in command of himself and those around him.

"Oh, I like your office clothes. A nice hands-off sort of style that I approve of wholeheartedly!" He grinned. "I don't want any other man getting the idea that you're available!"

Calla flushed. "Which any woman is unless she's been claimed by some male?"

"Uh-oh. I can see I blew that one," he muttered in self-disgust. "You know what I meant, honey. Don't try and twist my words. Please! I can't help it if I feel possessive toward you!"

"No, I don't suppose you can. It seems to be a problem a lot of men have. I'm ready to go, Slade."

The amber eyes glittered but he said nothing as he assisted her into the car and he kept the conversation carefully neutral on the drive to the posh town of Scottsdale, on the edge of Phoenix. He parked in the elegantly restored old town section and they walked past several of the expensive boutiques and galleries on the way to the restaurant. Not once during the entire time did Slade let the benign conversation falter.

It wasn't until they were seated in the dimly lit restaurant with its charming Spanish Colonial decor that Slade let the discussion become personal once more.

He reached for the leather case in his pocket, extracting the dark-rimmed glasses, and opened the menu with a curiously deliberate air.

"It's hard to believe this is our first dinner date," he remarked, his expression hidden by the oversized menu. "I feel like I've known you for so long . . ."

"An entire month," Calla joked casually, opening her own menu. The fingers of her right hand closed around the stem of her wineglass.

"That's a long time to want a woman and not ask her out!"

"Your restraint is commendable," she told him dryly, wondering where the new discussion was going.

"Oh, I can be patient enough when the goal is worth it," he told her calmly, closing the menu and removing his glasses.

"Doesn't it bother you at all to know that some women don't like being pursued as if they were a prize to be won and later discarded?"

"Tell me about him, Calla."

She set down the menu uneasily. "I don't like to talk about it, Slade."

86

"How will I be able to understand you if you don't tell me why you're letting your ex-husband still affect your life?" The words were calm, too calm.

Calla stared at him and was saved from an immediate answer when the waiter appeared to take their order. But the persistent, probing look in the amber eyes was still there when the waiter left with their order.

Suddenly a fierce urge to let this self-confident, determined man know exactly how hopeless his pursuit was took hold of her. Before she had time to think, Calla plunged into the short, sordid tale.

"All right, I'll tell you, Slade. Perhaps then you'll realize why I have no interest in getting involved with a man who treats a woman like prey!"

"Go ahead," he invited, lifting his wine glass and watching her thoughtfully. He didn't bother to deny the implied accusation.

"I met Drew Sheridan when I went to work for the same firm he worked at in Denver," she began tightly. "He was my boss. He soon let it be known he wanted to be more than my boss. He said he was in love with me. He was handsome, self-confident, successful, and all the other things a woman thinks she wants in a man. Including romantically possessive."

She broke off, half-waiting for some sort of justification of a man's right to be possessive. None came. There was a suspended look in Slade's expression. She couldn't tell what he was thinking.

"We were married. It wasn't the great passion I'd always dreamed of, but I was a realist. I knew, or I thought I knew, that good marriages are based on such things as mutual interests, mutual respect, and mutual trust. Drew and I had our work in common. I also thought we had the other two factors. Then I got promoted."

"And you started to become a threat?"

Calla nodded once. "I was no longer Drew's cute little protégée. Somehow, as far as he was concerned, I'd turned overnight into an aggressive, scheming, hard career woman who used men to get to the top. I was stunned. I'd actually been naive enough to think he'd be proud of me! But he was no longer my boss and that made all the difference. I was on a level with him."

"Things started coming apart at the seams?" Slade hazarded, still in an uncolored voice.

"At first it was just this sort of unspecific anger from him. And then he started complaining about the demands of my work. It didn't matter that his job made the same demands on him! For the sake of the marriage I started trying to get out of some of those demands. Predictably enough, my career began to suffer."

Calla paused, her mind's eye going back to that traumatic year in Denver. "I agreed, at the insistence of management, to go on a certain business trip. It was an essential one as far as the company was concerned. I came home to Drew's horrible accusations and innuendoes. He . . . he was in such a rage that he hit me." Calla closed her eyes and banished the memory with sheer willpower before she continued. "I promptly told the company I couldn't travel again. Drew naturally continued his traveling, often taking his secretary along. When I pointed out the unfairness of the arrangement and how my career was suffering for the sake of the marriage while his wasn't, he called me all sorts of horrible names and claimed it was 'natural' for a man to be *possessive* about his wife."

Calla sucked in a breath, her eyes narrowing. "I think he actually grew to hate me. Became obsessed with punishing me. Life became unbearable. Eventually I decided we had to come to some rational solution to the situation."

Her mouth twisted in self-mockery. "I thought it would be best to talk things over away from home and the office.

On neutral territory, so to speak. I got some time off and flew to meet him in Los Angeles, where he'd been attending a conference. I walked in and found Drew in bed with his secretary. I stood there like a fool and listened to my husband tell me it was all my fault. That I had driven him into the arms of another woman. That I was a cold, frigid female who didn't know the first thing about warming a man's bed or making him happy. And all the while his little blond secretary just lay there behind him and smiled at me. He told me he was going to marry her. I walked out of the room and filed for divorce. End of story."

She met Slade's eyes with cool defiance but he only responded with a quirking little smile.

"And the lesson you learned is that a man's possessiveness stems from an immature ego that can't abide a threatening woman. A possessive man is one who only wants his toy as long as he can dominate it completely. And when that toy can't be completely possessed, he goes in search of another one. Right?"

"It's not as if he was unique, Slade, and you know it. I think, from what I've seen during the past four years, that the majority of men are like him, at least the men I run into in the business world. They're not interested in building a lasting relationship with a woman who represents a threat to their egos. They have to dominate the relationship physically and economically or they want out of it, blaming the woman for ruining things."

"You were the one who warned me not to generalize about a group of men," Slade noted dryly.

"Do you deny your goal is to dominate our relationship?" she charged quietly.

"That question is loaded as hell and you know it!"

"A simple yes or no will do."

"There is no simple answer. You made the mistake of

89

marrying an immature boy and now you want to paint me as the same type."

"Can't you answer the question honestly?" she challenged boldly as the food was set before her.

Slade waited once again until the waiter had disappeared. She could see him exploring the trap she had set, looking for a way out. The thought that she'd managed to push him up against a wall gave Calla an unhappy satisfaction. Let him deny his instincts if he could!

"All right, Calla, I'll give you your answer," he finally said in soft roughness, his amber eyes clashing with her blue-green ones and holding them.

"Physically, yes, I want to make love to you in a way that will make you completely, unequivocally mine. I admit that could be termed possessive. I want to have you in my bed, hear you call my name in passion. I want to feel you shiver in my arms, beg for my kisses, my touch. And I want to tune your body so that it responds only to me!"

Calla felt the red color sweep up into her cheeks at his unequivocal words. Her fingers gripped the fork in her hand in an effort to still the trembling in them. She stared at him wordlessly.

"But," Slade continued intently, leaning forward, "I also want you to make love to me with the same fierceness! Do you understand?"

Calla said nothing, her face very still in the flickering candlelight as she tried to sort out the images in her mind.

"As far as the physical side of things goes, yes, I'm possessive. I think I'd want to kill any man who touched you after I'd made you mine. But I also want to be possessed!"

"Slade, please," Calla finally managed weakly. "This isn't the place for a discussion like this . . . !"

"You asked for it, you're going to get it," he told her

relentlessly. "Now about the economic side of things. That, frankly doesn't worry me. I've proven whatever I've had to prove to myself already. I know I'm capable of going farther and faster with York Instruments if that's what I want, but I've also got a sense of balance about life. I don't want my work to destroy me. I want time for my soaring, for lounging around a pool on a hot day, and most of all I want time for my woman. No, I wouldn't care if you got a job that paid as well as mine, but, yes, I would care if you weren't prepared to devote the same amount of energy and time to our marriage as I'm going to devote to it!"

"Slade, please keep your voice down," Calla begged helplessly, glancing nervously around the intimate dining room.

"But I haven't finished yet, Calla," he said silkily, waving a fork for emphasis. "There's something else you should know. If I discovered that my woman wasn't prepared to put me first in the same way that I intend to put her first, it would make me angry. I'll admit that I'd put my foot down—hard! But I sure as hell wouldn't start sleeping with another woman as a way of compensating or getting even! I don't fight like that!"

His declaration finally succeeded in goading Calla. She forgot about the danger of being overheard as she glared furiously across the table.

"Fine words, but what about the details? What happens if I have to travel in the course of my work? You've already tried to keep me from going off to Tucson next weekend!"

"Not because I don't trust you! But I don't like the idea of you being alone and unprotected around a lot of idiots who are on the make in a situation like that! And don't tell me there aren't plenty of them. I've been to enough 'seminars' and conferences to know!"

"What you're really saying is that you would be possessive to the point where it could hurt my career!"

"I'll be possessive, but I'm not irrational about it!" he snapped angrily. "Be reasonable, Calla. There aren't that many trips involved every year in work such as ours. I'll go with you on the necessary ones and I'll expect you to go with me when I travel. There may be occasions when that plan won't work out, but on the whole they should be few and far between if we limit our traveling to only the absolutely necessary trips! As long as we're both part of York Instruments," he added, smiling for the first time since he'd begun the tirade, "we should be able to control that part of our life very nicely."

"What you're really saying is that as long as I work for you, everything's nice and simple! You're still the one in charge!"

"You're really in a mood for a fight tonight, aren't you? Better eat your enchilada before it gets cold!"

The rest of the evening passed in a state of heightened tension for Calla. Slade refused to become involved in potentially dangerous topics, deliberately limiting the discussion to work, soaring, and other less emotional subjects. Calla's sense of self-discipline exerted itself and she followed his conversational lead with something like relief. It was as if they had both agreed upon a truce for the remainder of the meal.

But the tension persisted and on the way home it filled the intimate confines of the Mercedes.

"Will you kindly relax?" Slade finally said whimsically as he slowed for a light. "You feel like a coiled spring sitting beside me!"

"Not unexpected, perhaps, when you consider what happened last night after you took me home!" she remarked sardonically, gazing deliberately out the window.

"You have my word: no more judo if you refrain from

swinging at me with a candlestick! Besides, I already told you this morning I'm going to try and handle you with kid gloves, remember? You don't have to be afraid I'll force myself on you, sweetheart."

"I'm not afraid of you, Slade. But I do prefer to avoid scenes such as the one you created last night!"

"Understood," he said obligingly as he halted the car in her parking lot. "I shall treat you as if you were made out of the finest and most delicate porcelain," he vowed. "If that's really what you want!" he went on to add with a laughing leer.

"It's what I want," she confirmed loftily as he walked her toward the door. "The question is, are you capable of restraining yourself that well?"

"Try me. Invite me in for a cup of coffee."

"That's how things started last night."

"Okay, make it tea. Or brandy. Perhaps I'll get drunk and pass out harmlessly on your couch."

Calla knew she was responding to the humor in him and surrendered. He really did look quite harmless tonight. And he'd behaved himself reasonably well all day.

"I have," she drawled slowly as she handed him her key, "some very good cognac. I don't pour it for just anyone, you understand . . ."

"I shall treat it with reverence," Slade promised, eyes gleaming with laughter.

Fifteen minutes later, the cognac warming from the heat of their hands cupped around the snifters, Slade stared down into the shimmering liquid and said very neutrally, "Come with me to Sedona tomorrow. We've still got two days left in the weekend." He was talking about the colorful arts and crafts oriented town near the Oak Creek Canyon, an attraction for visitors and residents alike.

Calla sipped her cognac. "If you're asking me to spend the night with you in Sedona, the answer is no."

He nodded moodily. "I was afraid it might be. But it was worth a try." He set down his snifter and turned to face her as she sat beside him on the couch. "Well, since I'm not going to be allowed to jump ahead a few squares on the board, I suppose I'd better start working from where I am."

He reached out and removed her glass of cognac, putting it down beside his on the table. Very gently he put his hands on her shoulders.

Calla stiffened, meeting his eyes firmly. "Slade, you promised . . ."

"I promised not to rush you or force myself on you," he agreed, pulling her toward him with exquisite tenderness. "But that doesn't mean," he went on, his mouth hovering barely an inch above hers, "that I can't beg, plead, coax, or sell my soul for a kiss, does it?"

"Oh, Slade!" Calla whispered, not knowing how to respond to the new gentleness in him.

He didn't answer. His mouth came down on hers in the lightest of feathering caresses and Calla's eyes fluttered shut in reaction.

Warm, soft, inviting, persuasive, his lips moved on hers. There was no overwhelming male aggression in him tonight. Gradually Calla began to relax. What had happened last night had been unnerving and alarming, arousing emotions in her she hadn't even guessed she'd been capable of. Emotions Drew had never seemed to seek or to want.

But tonight everything was soft and gentle. Tonight there was no threat, no need to defend herself physically or emotionally. Calla knew she could stop Slade in a second. All she had to do was withdraw or make some definite protest.

The unexpected sense of safety soothed and lulled, enfolding Calla deeper and deeper even as her body began to awaken to a need to be enfolded in Slade's arms.

But he made no move to draw her closer against his hardness, letting his mouth nibble with incredible lightness at the corners of her own.

"I love to feel your lips when they begin to grow soft under mine," he breathed in a deep voice of closely leashed passion. "It's like kissing a flower whose petals unfold at the proper touch."

The warmth of him began to become a tangible pull on Calla's senses and she shifted slightly under his hands. A kind of deep, inner restlessness flickered to life in the pit of her stomach.

Beneath the velvet coaxing of his mouth her lips parted, allowing him the more intimate contact for which he pleaded. Calla was leaning against the support of his fingers on her shoulders now, her body inclining toward his of its own accord as it began to enjoy the taste of the safe, gentle lovemaking.

"Calla, my sweet. You're all honey and fire, do you know that?"

She felt the trembling in him and marveled at it. Had he trembled last night and had she not been aware of it because there was so much she'd been wary of? And what did he mean about her being made of honey and fire? She knew she wasn't like that. Drew had made that very, very clear . . .

Calla moaned softly, a tiny sigh deep in her throat. The need for more of his warmth was prodding her forward against the restraint of his hands. Her fingers hesitated and then touched the knot of his tie. Slade's jacket had been removed when he'd accepted the cognac.

"Yes, please!" he growled as she almost unconsciously began loosening the gold and brown striped tie.

Calla heard the male need in him, felt it in the tautened muscles of his arms, and waited breathlessly for him to slide the fingers on her shoulders around to the zipper of her dress.

He made no such move and after an expectant moment she went on with the sensuous business of unraveling his tie. She felt the tip of his tongue in her ear when at last the tie hung open around his neck. The wet, warm caress sent a shiver through her system.

Calla heard her own soft moan as her hand dropped to the strength of his smoothly muscled leg. There was an answering groan from him and, of their own volition, her fingers began moving up the length of his thigh in a series of circles that climbed higher and higher. It was like soaring, she thought dazedly.

And then he moved a matter of inches on the leather couch and her hand was thrust into contact with the male hardness of him. Calla recoiled as if she were a sailplane pilot who had flown too close to the sun.

"Slade!" she gasped, every nerve violently alive and fiercely aware of his desire. With shaking tension she waited for him to pull her into his arms. It was what he wanted to do, she was certain of it. He wanted to touch her as he had touched her last night. Wanted to possess her . . .

But he did nothing of the kind. His hands tightened slightly on her shoulders and she felt his breath quicken as he nuzzled the sensitive skin behind her ear, but he made no move to give way to the instincts which must have been driving him.

"Slade?" Her voice was a tiny, questioning whisper of sound as her fingers rose to the first button of his yellow shirt.

"Don't you understand, Calla?" he rasped in an agonized masculine need. "I want you to claim me for your

96

lover tonight. I want you to possess me as surely as I will be possessing you. I want you to learn what possession really means between a man and a woman; that it has nothing to do with the neurotic, self-centered emotion you knew in your ex-husband!"

CHAPTER SIX

Calla stared up into the amber eyes and desperately asked herself how things could have come to such a point. What in the world was the matter with her? Where was her painfully acquired discipline and self-control? *And above all, why was it this man!*

"What's the matter, sweetheart?" Slade murmured on the merest thread of humor. "Are you changing your mind about what you want tonight? Does that wary look in those oceans you call eyes mean you're not going to pick me up and carry me off to bed after all?"

"Oh, Slade, you big idiot!" she gasped, surrendering to the laughter that welled up in response to the image he'd created. "I doubt if I could get you down the hall even if I were to try dragging you by the heels!"

"Sure you could. People carry people off to bed all the time. I have it on the best authority."

"Uh-huh. But the way I hear it, it's the man who carries the woman off in his arms!" she retorted with a mocking little grin. It was astonishing, she thought light-headedly, how unafraid she was. The banter seemed to increase her small store of confidence even further. She would never have teased Drew like this . . .

"Well, I suppose I could volunteer to assist in my own seduction," Slade opined thoughtfully. "But it does seem a bit unfair somehow."

"You can relax! I have no intention of seducing you and even less of carrying you off to bed."

"No?" He gave her a regretful look. "Then would you please tease me some more?"

"Tease you!"

"Umm. I know a man isn't supposed to like being sexually teased, but when it's all he can get from his woman . . ."

He bent his head once more, his eyes hooded and enticing as he resumed the slow, languorous kiss that seemed to do nothing so much as invite her response.

Calla felt herself slip back under the spell much more quickly this time, her fingers straying to the button she hadn't quite undone earlier.

As soon as the fastening parted, her hand slid down to the next and the next as if it had a mind of its own. Her fingertips ran lightly through the rough, curling hair of his chest, glorying in the primitive thrill.

She heard his muttered plea for more of her touch and then somehow she had forced her way past the restraining influence of his grip on her shoulders to snuggle against his chest and run her arms around his waist inside the open shirt. His muscled back was taut and strong and fairly demanded the kneading of her nails.

"Oh, my God, Calla!" Slade muttered huskily.

She nestled in the crook of his arm, her lips nibbling now at his throat and the curve of his shoulder. The tingling warmth that had come alive in her body was spreading, radiating out to the farthest reaches, and creating a longing drive that was different from anything she had ever known. She recognized the pulse of desire and knew at once it went beyond anything she had ever had with Drew . . .

Slade was using his fingers lightly, teasingly on the back of her neck, sending more of the shocking little shivers down her spine. She felt his lips take the place of his fingers and knew his hand had gone at last to the zipper of the turquoise and white dress.

Once again she waited, expectant, and, yes, eager. Once

again his hand didn't follow through with the wished-for action.

Her nails bit deeply into the skin above his waist, conveying her growing frustration. She sagged against him heavily as the small punishment made him draw in his breath sharply. Didn't he know what she wanted? He must know!

"Slade, please!" she whispered hoarsely, twisting against him like a small cat begging to be stroked.

She felt his teeth very lightly, very tantalizingly on her nape, and then the zipper began to slide down.

Using the only means she had of encouraging him, Calla slipped the yellow shirt from his shoulders, and when she went back into his arms with a small cry of delight, he finally returned the favor. The top of the dress was lowered slowly to her waist.

"Such a beautiful body!" Slade's voice was thick with the desire and need Calla found herself longing to hear in it.

"Touch me, Slade. Please touch me!"

He held her in one arm, her head on his shoulder, and touched the tip of her small, rounded breast with tenderness and teasing passion. It wasn't enough.

With her hands clasped tightly around the column of his neck, Calla leaned forward, using her slighter weight to push him back until he lay flat on the couch beneath her. Feeling incredibly abandoned and deliciously wanton, she let her nipples graze his chest while she nuzzled his throat and then the tip of his ear.

"Are you trying to drive me crazy?"

"Yes!" she breathed, closing her teeth a little fiercely around his earlobe. "Oh, yes!"

His large, strong hands slid down her back, pushing the dress over the curve of her buttocks and then impelling her hips deeply into his.

She gasped at the intimate contact and buried her face in his neck.

"Do you want me, Slade?" she whispered, and trembled as his fingers slid just inside the waistband of her lacy briefs.

"That's a foolish question," he grated harshly, gently clenching the soft flesh of her buttocks. "I want you more than anything else on this earth!"

"Yes," she panted, and couldn't have said whether the word was one of surrender or sheer feminine satisfaction.

"Do you want me, Calla?"

She hesitated a fraction of a second but realized dimly she was too far gone in the chaotic world of physical sensation to lie.

"I want you, Slade."

"I'm yours, sweetheart," he said softly.

She raised her head to look down at him and his hands slid up her waist and ribs and stopped at the pointed breasts. His thumbs moved delicately, coaxingly on the peaking nipples.

She arched against him in response, her legs, still wrapped in the folds of the dress, gliding along the insides of his. Her sandals had fallen soundlessly to the carpet and now her toes curled in primitive reaction to the electricity coiling through her body.

"All yours," he repeated, bending one leg slightly to trap her restless ankle. The amber eyes flamed up into hers. "Are you going to accept the gift?"

"I . . . I don't know . . ."

Panic began to grow as a distant alarm warned Calla matters were slipping out of control much too rapidly. It wasn't an overriding fear yet, but the first uncertainties were there. It struck her forcibly that things would be much simpler if Slade stopped talking and made love to her. If he were just a little more aggressive she could blank out this sense of having to make a choice. No, no, she didn't want that! Because then Slade would find out the truth. He would learn that she wasn't any good at pleasing a man and right now Calla couldn't bear that prospect.

"In that case, I take back my gift!"

"What?" Dazedly, Calla stared down at him, confused, and upset by the confusion.

"You heard me. I'm not giving myself to a woman who won't reach out and take me with both hands and every ounce of her willpower. I like to think I'm worth more than a lukewarm 'maybe'!"

"Slade! What are you talking about?"

"I want you to want me so much that nothing on earth could stop you," he told her, eyes glinting with intent. "I want to be swept off my feet, taken, possessed, chained to you with ropes of steel. Don't you understand yet? That's how badly I want you! But until you can want me in the same way, I'll get by on cold showers!"

Gently but quite forcefully he set her aside and got to his feet, reaching for the discarded yellow shirt. He turned to spear her with his golden gaze as he tugged it on. Deliberately he let the amber fire roam her almost nude body and she felt scorched by the heat.

Something deep inside Calla reacted to that look. He did want her! It was costing him a great effort to walk away from her tonight. With a little provocation on her part she could make him stay.

But what if she convinced him to stay and then he later turned away from her unsatisfied? The way Drew had so often done?

Calla shut her eyes for an instant against that awful possibility and when she opened them again, Slade was at the door.

"Good night, Calla," he said quietly over his shoulder, and then he was gone.

103

For several moments longer she sat curled on the couch, crushing the folds of the turquoise and white dress that lay in a heap beneath her. It was a warm night; but when he'd left, Slade had taken the heat from the room.

Calla felt the dampness stinging her eyes as she eventually pulled herself with surprising awkwardness to her feet. She stood forlornly for a minute, trying to readjust her thoughts.

What had she done by allowing Slade York this close? Hadn't she learned anything about possessive, domineering men four years ago? How could she be such a fool as to find herself on the brink of falling in love with another one?

Falling in love! Calla swallowed heavily at the horrifying thought. No, it wasn't possible. She would not play the fool again! But even as she assured herself of that, a nagging little voice insisted on pointing out that things were different enough this time to make matters dangerous.

If Slade had been *exactly* like Drew, Calla told herself sadly as she headed for her bedroom, there would have been no problem. She could never confront a man *exactly* like Drew again with any other feeling than one of loathing and contempt.

But Slade wasn't like Drew. He was an altogether different man. Except, Calla reminded herself firmly, for his possessiveness, his promise of being a jealous husband.

No! She would not go through that kind of frightening marriage again! Especially not for the lure of discovering the joy of physical satisfaction! One didn't marry for sex! And, she admitted to herself, as she stood in front of the bedroom mirror, she couldn't abide the possibility of Slade not finding complete satisfaction in her arms. A man like that would demand everything of a woman. And if she couldn't give it . . . ?

Calla shook her head to clear it of the depressing

thoughts, turning away from the mirror and struggling into a nightgown. She was in control of her own life now. She had the self-discipline to get through the current turmoil!

But just before she went to bed, Calla had a vision of trying to resist Slade's tantalizing gift for the next three months. How much willpower did she really have? Ruefully, she acknowledged she had never been faced with quite this sort of temptation and fell into a fitful sleep.

The next morning Calla arose with the determination and restored sense of perspective she felt had been sadly lacking the previous evening. There was only one person who could put life back on an even keel, restore the order and quiet routine of her days, and that was herself.

With renewed vigor, she set about cleaning her oven, a chore guaranteed to make even the most depressed woman lose herself in physical exertion. She was up to her elbows in suds and grease when the doorbell chimed.

With a sigh and a pained groan, she got up from her knees and went to answer the summons.

"Slade! What are you doing here?"

She stared at him in astonishment. During the night he had become an inimical, larger than life figure to her subconscious mind. A man to be treated with great wariness and mistrust. And now here he stood before her smiling with easy warmth and friendliness. It was difficult reconciling the two images, and it was the dangerous one that cracked and then shattered. In the bright sunlight of midday, her mind could accept only the Slade who stood on her doorstep.

"How does fettuccine and a glass of red wine sound?" He grinned, surveying her soiled and rumpled figure.

She wrinkled her nose thoughtfully, aware of suds dripping lightly to the tile beneath her feet. "That depends on who's doing the cooking."

"You are looking at one of the greatest Italian chefs of all time," he informed her nonchalantly.

"That's funny, you don't look Italian."

"Which only goes to show that great cooking knows no ethnic boundaries," he chuckled smoothly. "Shall we leave now or do you want to finish playing mudpies first?"

"You are looking at one of the great housekeepers of all time. I'm cleaning my oven!"

"That's funny, you don't look like a drudge."

"Which only goes to show that great housekeeping knows no single personality type!"

"I'll wait while you clean up and put on a fresh shirt," he said blandly, stepping over the threshold and forcing her back into the hall with no apparent effort. "What is that weapon in your hand?"

"That's a scrubbing pad. I don't suppose you'd like to help finish my oven, would you?" she asked interestedly, turning to walk briskly back toward the kitchen.

"Boy, are you perceptive! I had the intelligence and foresight to get a self-cleaning oven. Marry me and I'll let you have it as a wedding present."

Calla flashed him a quick glance, uncertain of his mood. But the amber gaze was smiling and there was no indication of anything other than gentle teasing in his face.

"You're too generous!"

"Well, the same strings are attached to the oven as are attached to me," he admitted. "You really have to *want* both of us. My oven has its pride, too!"

Calla refused to let him disconcert her. She was back in charge of herself this morning, dammit! "A real self-cleaning oven, hmm?" she asked, as if thinking the matter over in great depth.

"Just turn a couple of knobs and lock the door. Nary

a scrubbing pad needed for the rest of your life. Attractive package, isn't it? And you can acquire it practically free."

"Except for the attached strings, of course."

"Well, there is no completely free lunch," he reminded her studiously.

Wiping off the remaining soap and grime from the oven door, Calla almost flinched at the words. No such thing as a free lunch.

"Are you trying to tell me something?" she demanded wryly, concentrating on her chore.

"Sure," he said agreeably. "I'm telling you there's no such thing as a free marriage. Not with me."

She flicked a glance at him as he stood lounging in the doorway. "How about the fettuccine? What's the price on it?"

"Same as the one on me and the self-cleaning oven. You really have to want it. None of us wants lukewarm appreciation, you see."

Calla rinsed out the scrubbing pad and then swiveled to face him, her hands resting on either side of her against the sink. She watched his face for a moment, her thoughts churning. The safest thing to do was to throw him out.

"I really do like fettuccine," she finally said slowly.

"A lot?"

▶ "I love it."

"In that case, it's all yours. Come and get it."

Twenty minutes later, Calla found herself looking forward with an unexpected curiosity to seeing Slade's home. Some of the eagerness must have showed because Slade slanted her a laughing glance as he parked the Mercedes in the drive of a sleek, white modern structure with a red tile roof. An expanse of windows and a courtyard gave it an airy look.

"You approve?" he demanded laconically as she surveyed the palms and sweep of green lawn.

"It's very lovely," she nodded. "But what I really came to see was the oven!"

He laughed, leading the way past a handsome wrought-iron gate and into the brick courtyard. The inside of the house, Calla realized at once as the door swung open, was as cool and airy as the outside. The furniture was an eclectic combination that could only be described as Western Modern. It was designed for comfort but there was a rugged quality to it that carried the stamp of its owner.

"The oven is right through here," Slade said importantly, guiding her across the hardwood floor with its distinctive scattering of Indian rugs. The kitchen proved large, functional, and pleasantly rustic.

"It's beautiful," Calla said, studying the self-cleaning oven with an entranced expression.

"Just wait," he promised, stepping around her to open a pantry door. "I have lots of other assets with which to woo you!"

"Your cooking?"

"My great Italian cooking," he corrected, hauling the pasta out of the cupboard.

When they finally sat down to lunch on the patio, Calla had to admit he had a point.

"You're wasting your talents running York Instruments. You should open a restaurant!"

"Then it would be work, not a hobby," he explained as if she weren't very bright.

"And you like to keep the two separate and distinct?"

"I've told you, I want a balanced life."

Calla thought about that. "I think I live a . . . a focused life," she found herself saying in a strange little voice after a minute. "Your outside activities like soaring and cooking all seem completely separate from one another. You enjoy each independently of the other. Whereas with me, I do things that tend to reinforce each other."

"You mean, things that reinforce your sense of inner strength, don't you?" he asked calmly, helping himself to another roll. "You've created an inner core of steel and you're determined to never again bend it for any man, aren't you?"

She shook her head. "No, it's not that simple. You're looking at it from a typically masculine viewpoint. A woman who won't submit herself to a man is an affront to every male ego. You see relationships in terms of a power structure. Someone has to dominate. But I'm looking for something different . . ."

"You're looking for a man you can dominate?" He grinned cheerfully, stuffing the roll politely into his mouth and chewing enthusiastically.

"No! I'm looking for an open, honest, and even relationship. One in which each partner completely trusts the other and has no wish to change him or her."

"Forget it. Such a relationship doesn't exist, except for two people who are living together as roommates!"

"I disagree. I think there are men in the world who are capable of treating a woman as an equal in every sense of the word!" Calla announced loftily.

"Equality has nothing to do with passion!" he informed her, pouring more of the Italian red wine into her glass. "A passionate relationship demands that both parties give and take, make changes in their lives, and, yes, for a woman like you, it's going to mean learning to live with my possessiveness."

"Never!"

He grinned wickedly. "Wait and see. I'm going to show you a side of yourself you never even knew you had!"

"Is that a threat?" Calla demanded rashly, not feeling in the least concerned out here in the warm sunshine. The world seemed too pleasant just then to pay much attention to threats.

"Definitely."

They spent the afternoon, on Calla's whimsical suggestion, at the Heard Museum, with its fabulous collection of primitive art and anthropological exhibits. American Indian basketry and pottery together with sophisticated archaeological evidence told the story of twenty-five thousand years of Indian history in Arizona. Slade seemed as interested as she did in the displays, and somehow the afternoon slipped pleasantly through their fingers.

When he took her home that evening, Slade left her on the doorstep with only a light, fleeting kiss. He offered her no chance to pursue the strange exploration she had begun on Saturday night and Calla found herself biting her lip in silent frustration as he waved good-bye and climbed into the Mercedes. He could have at least kissed her a little more thoroughly!

The thought brought her back to reality in a hurry. What in the world did she mean by that? Calla went to bed angry with herself and annoyed at Slade.

Taking Monday off from work, they went swimming together, enjoying tall glasses of lemonade by the condominium pool. It was a slightly unnerving experience for Calla to be able to study Slade's hard, smoothly muscled body at her leisure. And she winced inwardly at one point when he rose, dripping, from the water and caught her blue-green eyes on him.

"Like what you see?" He grinned, self-confident and assured in his masculinity.

"Bathing trunks that small ought to be outlawed," she informed him haughtily.

His eyes swept over her figure in its green maillot and laughed. "Funny, I was just thinking how nice it would be to go without any swimming suits at all!"

"The neighbors would have a fit."

110

"What about you? Would you be willing if it weren't for the neighbors?"

"You'll never know, will you?" she taunted, lowering her lashes and leaning her head back against the lounger.

"Yes, I will. I've got a swimming pool in my own backyard, you know. Totally shielded from prying eyes. Someday I'll invite you over for a swim and we'll find out how uninhibited you really are!"

"I shall be very careful about accepting any more invitations to your house," she chuckled as he sat down on the lounger next to her.

From under her lashes she watched him towel the water off his broad, tanned shoulders. A strong man. Lean and rugged and coordinated. Heavy, too, she thought with an inner grin. And he wanted her to carry him off to bed!

"You have ballet class this evening?" Slade asked, settling back and shutting his dark lashes against the sun.

"Umm."

"What time do you get out?"

"Six."

"Take a change of clothes with you. I'll drive you to class and pick you up after. We can have dinner."

"Are you planning on occupying all my evenings during this, uh, courtship?" Calla asked distantly, not quite certain how to react to the command.

He turned his head on the lounger to stare into her eyes, his coffee-dark hair sleekly water-tousled. "Every one I can get," he confirmed seriously.

Calla contented herself with an arched eyebrow but she didn't refuse his evening plans.

But when she emerged, soaking wet with perspiration and her muscles tired from Miss Marsden's demands, Calla knew a certain sense of anticipation. She was almost afraid to glance out into the lobby area of the studio in case Slade hadn't arrived.

111

She was so anxiously searching for him in the seating area that she didn't see him until he spoke in her ear.

"Does she always yell at you like that?" he asked, indicating Miss Marsden, who was still in the studio, discussing technique with a student.

"Keep your voice down!" Calla insisted in a fierce whisper. "No, she doesn't always yell at me like that." She grinned. "Sometimes she yells much more loudly! She was actually rather pleased with me tonight."

The stream of women in black leotards and buns ebbed and flowed around them as they stood to one side of the entrance to the dance studio. Slade ignored the surreptitious glances from the other women and stared at Calla in astonishment.

"If I yelled at you like that at work, you'd raise hell!"

Calla lifted her chin regally, but her eyes were twinkling as she told him airily, "Miss Marsden is a mistress of the ballet!"

"And that makes it okay?"

"It certainly does!"

"I shall have to talk to her. I could use her secret!"

"Don't bother. It wouldn't work outside ballet class. Demanding, temperamental instructors are part of the mystique, you see. One expects it of them."

"I still think I could make a first-rate manager out of her!"

"You probably could, but she'd rather starve than abandon the ballet!"

"Oh, well, I have you. Maybe some of her management technique will rub off on her student! Run along and get dressed. I'm hungry."

"Calla, old friend, old dancing buddy! What have you been hiding from me?" Angie Connors demanded with a knowing grin as Calla slipped into the changing room and began peeling off her leotard in preparation for a shower.

"If I had someone like that waiting for me after dance class . . . !" She broke off to make a purring sound and kissed the tips of her fingers expressively.

"He's my new boss," Calla began, trying to defuse the situation. She really didn't feel like trying to explain Slade to anyone. Especially not another woman.

"Why don't any of my bosses ever look like that! All male jungle cat!"

Calla laughed helplessly. "Angie, your imagination is incredible. I didn't even think he was particularly handsome!"

"He's not. What's that got to do with it?" Angie murmured.

With a rueful sigh, Calla stepped beneath the shower, determined not to discuss Slade any further. She wasn't sure why, but she didn't like seeing that look in another woman's eyes. Something deep inside rebelled at it. Something that hadn't been upset when other women had looked at Drew. . . .

Dressed in a pair of jeans and a bright green shirt that deepened the color of her eyes, Calla slipped into her sandals and tossed her leotard and tights into a small bag with her ballet slippers. She checked her neat head in the mirror, slung the leather strap of the bag over her shoulder, and sauntered back into the lobby area, thinking about dinner and Slade York.

The sight that greeted her as she walked out of the dressing room relegated her hunger to the bottom of her list of priorities.

Slade stood talking to Gary Crispin and both men had that wary, faintly challenging attitude that men have when they are talking about a woman they both want. There was no sign of open hostilities but Calla, nevertheless, felt like a bone thrown between two large dogs.

Which was absolutely ridiculous, she told herself resolutely, starting forward determinedly. Gary was a friend, nothing more. And Slade? Well, Slade needed to learn a few manners!

"Hello, Gary," she began crisply, adopting an in-charge tone. "I see you've met Slade."

"You seem to have brought those negotiations you were conducting to a very favorable conclusion," Gary said, his dark eyes meeting hers with an enigmatic expression she'd never before seen in them.

"Oh, rest assured, she has me eating out of the palm of her hand," Slade murmured, his amber gaze following Gary's dark one to rest on Calla's disciplined features. "And speaking of eating, if you'll excuse us, we're on our way to dinner."

"Of course," Gary said formally.

"Slade was very impressed with Miss Marsden," Calla said, trying for a light note. "He's talking of stealing her away and making a manager out of her!"

"Surely Mr. York doesn't expect me to give up so easily?" Gary mocked sardonically, watching as Slade put a proprietary arm around Calla's shoulders.

"Mr. York," Slade said gently, "has what he wants. He'll let you keep Miss Marsden."

Without another word, he led Calla toward the door, his grip on her shoulders deceptively casual. Only she could feel the way his fingers were biting into the flesh beneath the green shirt.

"Slade, please, you're hurting me!" she muttered in annoyance as they walked toward the Mercedes parked near the curb. She attempted to move out from under his arm and found herself unable to do so.

"It's nothing compared to what I'm tempted to do!" he growled. "I want your word of honor you'll never see that man outside of ballet class!"

Calla felt her temper ignite. "Why, Slade York! I

thought a man like you didn't worry about a male ballet dancer encroaching on his private preserves!"

"I'm glad you realize you're private property," he shot back, sliding behind the wheel. "Now, let me have your promise."

CHAPTER SEVEN

"I see no reason why I should give you my word on a matter like this," Calla began imperiously as Slade started the Mercedes and pulled away from the curb with a frowning glance into the side mirror. "My relationship with Gary is strictly my business!"

Calla considered his hard profile for a moment, a strange curiosity driving her next question.

"What if I were to tell you that Gary and I are merely friends? That our 'relationship' has never gone beyond the classroom? That he sent the flowers simply because he was a friend who knew I was involved with a difficult situation at work?"

"Are you telling me all that?" Slade retorted coolly, flicking an amber glance across the seat at her cold, withdrawn expression.

"Yes."

He shrugged. "In that case, I believe you."

"You do?" Calla was somewhat flustered. Drew would never have believed her in a million years. He would have ranted and raved and accused her of having a sordid affair. He would have called her every name in the book. . . .

"But that doesn't change anything," Slade went on evenly. "I still want your promise not to see him outside the school."

"You just said you believed me when I told you I wasn't having an affair!" Calla cried in angry frustration. He was exactly like Drew after all! He would never trust her!

"I do believe you, honey," he said quietly. "But I want your word, nevertheless."

"Why?" she demanded starkly.

He sighed. "Isn't it obvious? You're an adult, Calla. Haven't you learned by now that any friendship between a man and a woman carries with it the risk of one of the two wanting something more? Whatever you've had with Crispin, I can guarantee he's starting to want more out of it. I'm a man, Calla. Give me some credit for understanding my own sex!"

"But Gary's never said or done anything to indicate he wants anything more than a friendship with me!" she protested.

"Perhaps he didn't even realize what he wanted until he saw you walk away with me tonight. Some men are like that."

Unhappily Calla recalled her initial impression on seeing the two men talking quietly in the waiting area of the academy. Like two dogs on the verge of quarreling over a bone . . .

"Calla, both of us should have learned that a marriage is a delicate structure that must be treated with care and respect. A man and a woman owe that much to each other when they agree to live together, don't you admit?"

"Yes, but you and I haven't reached any sort of agreement!"

"You've agreed to let me court you," he reminded her blandly. "That means you're thinking about marriage. And that means you ought to be willing to refrain from encouraging other men."

"Slade," she said in a distant tone, her eyes focused on the passing scenery, "do you really believe me when I tell you I'm not having an affair with Gary?"

He threw her a somewhat surprised glance. "I told you I did."

She chewed her lower lip thoughtfully and said nothing.

"What's the big deal about that?" he went on and then

broke off to nod in sudden understanding. "Oh, I get it. Your ex-husband wouldn't have believed you, is that it? Well, to tell you the truth, if you were my ex-wife, I wouldn't believe you, either!" There was a wry note of something less than amusement in his voice.

"Tell me about her, Slade," Calla heard herself say impulsively. "I've told you a lot about Drew."

He hesitated and then lifted a hand in negligent response. "Why not? If you're sure you want to hear it. A fairly simple tale, really."

He told her over dinner in a Polynesian restaurant. When she had first arrived in Phoenix Calla had found the idea of a South Seas restaurant something of an anomaly in the desert. But she had later learned that the state boasted more boats per capita than anywhere else in the world. There must be something about living in the desert that made a person appreciate water!

She sipped a Mai Tai, toying idly with the speared fruit in the glass, and listened without comment until Slade had finished his story.

"It's hard on man's ego to find out his wife didn't marry him for himself but for the things he represented. Looking back on it, I suppose I'd have to say my marriage was a business proposition from start to finish. Sheila was very beautiful and I guess I was flattered when she showed signs of being interested in me. I hate to admit this but she was my secretary."

Slade's mouth twisted wryly at the confession. "A classic office romance, I suppose. But she had looks and charm and a sophistication that seemed just right for the kind of wife I felt I needed at the time. I, in turn, represented financial security, a foot on the rung of a ladder she wanted very badly to start climbing. She liked very much the idea of being married to an up-and-coming young businessman who was making a mark in the community. She

119

also liked the idea of bridge and drinks at the country club at two in the afternoon, dancing and little flirtations at the country club in the evening, and the possibility of living a jet-setting sort of life-style."

Calla waited while he sipped his drink, aware of a fierce unhappiness that Slade had been through such a painful experience. She wanted to comfort him and it took an effort to shake off the urge to soothe and make him forget.

"To put it simply," Slade went on ruefully, "I'm not exactly the jet-setting type. I didn't share Sheila's social instincts. I wanted a quieter life with a woman who wanted to be with me just because she wanted *me*. Fortunately for both of us, Sheila found someone at the country club who shared her outlook on life. Several someones, I gather," he added bleakly. "At any rate, she eventually left me to marry a man who could advance her considerably higher on the social ladder. And that's the whole story in a nutshell. We were married less than two years."

"Does she still live in Phoenix?" Calla asked hesitantly.

"No. She and her husband had moved to Los Angeles, last I heard, why?"

"Just curious."

"You don't have to be afraid of running into her accidentally, you know. You and I won't be frequenting the sort of places Sheila cares for even if she were still in town," Slade assured her with a small grin.

Calla drew a deep breath and asked cautiously, "Did you feel possessive about Sheila?"

Slade frowned grimly. "No man likes the idea of his wife sleeping around," he said arrogantly. "But when I found out about it, my emotion was to end the marriage. She very kindly made the first move and took care of the legalities, however. Now, with you, my emotions would be entirely different!"

Calla's eyes narrowed. "What do you mean by that?"

120

"I mean that if I were to find out you were interested in another man I wouldn't calmly go out and file for divorce," he told her in a deep, gritty voice that suddenly roughened dangerously. "I'd drag you home by the hair and then chain you on such a short leash you wouldn't be able to go any farther away than the kitchen or the bedroom!"

"Slade!" she hissed, flushing under his glittering, intent gaze. "Don't talk like that! It makes you sound . . ."

"A little primitive?" he suggested.

"Very primitive!"

"Which brings us back to Crispin," he retorted smoothly, watching her startled expression. "Thought I'd forgotten all about that, didn't you?"

"Why not?" she managed glibly, stirring her Mai Tai again with an air of great industriousness. "Last night you forgot to discuss my upcoming little trip to Tucson!"

"I merely postponed that conversation. Now, about Crispin . . ."

Calla eyed his implacable expression from behind the shelter of slightly lowered lashes. Idly her fingers drummed soundlessly on the white tablecloth while she ran the situation over and over in her mind.

"You can sort through all the possible avenues of escape, but I can tell you right now there's no point wasting your time. I'm only going to be satisfied with one answer," he drawled.

"My promise not to see Gary outside of class?"

"You've got it in one," he mocked.

"Well, why not?" Calla abruptly declared with the air of one making a major concession out of the goodness of her heart. "I haven't dated Gary in the past three months so I suppose I can wait another three months!"

"You're functioning under the impression the courtship won't be successful?" Slade asked blandly.

"How did you guess?" She smiled brilliantly.

"Don't think," he warned with an answering smile that was extremely wolfish in nature, "that just because you held me at bay over the negotiating table that I haven't got some hidden talents!"

That evening when he took her home, it was only a fierce self-honesty that compelled Calla to admit to herself the real reason she invited Slade in for cognac. She didn't want him sliding back into the Mercedes with only a casual good-bye kiss on the doorstep again!

What was the matter with her? she demanded silently, carrying the snifters back into the living room. Talk about playing with fire! But surely a little of his warmth and strength wasn't too much to take tonight? She was thirty years old. Didn't she have the right to some physical excitement with a man who could ruffle her nerve endings just by looking at her?

She would be very careful, she assured herself as she sat down beside him on the couch and met the golden gaze over the rim of the glass. She would only allow herself a kiss or two. He should be willing enough, after all. Wasn't Slade under the impression this was a genuine courtship?

But Slade made no obvious move, merely chatting quietly as he leaned back against the couch, feet outstretched and his collar unbuttoned. He looked utterly relaxed and there was a lazy provocation in the amber eyes. But he didn't reach out and initiate the gentle lovemaking.

Calla took another swallow of cognac and considered her next move. He must know she wanted to kiss him. He seemed to know so much about her already! She remembered what he'd said about wanting to be swept off his feet. What he was really saying, of course, was that he wanted to know she truly wanted him. And who could blame him after that awful experience with his ex-wife!

It was that notion that finally gave Calla the courage to

set down her cognac snifter and somehow manage to brush his leg with her hand in the process. And once having voluntarily touched him, it became much easier.

"Well?" he prompted gently as her fingertips rested lightly on the fabric of his slacks. "What are you waiting for? Don't you want to kiss me?"

"You," she stated with great dignity, "are an arrogant, provoking, utterly unprincipled male!"

"But you want me anyway, don't you?" he said softly, tantalizingly.

"I don't know," she replied with total honesty. "But I would like very much to kiss you once or twice before you go home tonight."

"Aren't you afraid a couple of kisses might lead to bed and me not going home at all?" he asked whimsically.

"No."

"I'm in for another night of teasing?"

"Are you objecting?" she asked boldly, her smile very ancient in origin. It was a smile of female invitation and promise as old as the hills and as young as the moment.

"If I did object," he breathed on a whisper as she bent her head close to his, "what would you do?"

"The issue doesn't arise," she advised him recklessly. "You'll take what you can get, remember?"

"You are a hard-hearted woman," he complained just before her lips came down on his.

It was easier tonight, much easier. And Calla refused to recognize the danger in the soft seductiveness of his restrained response. Seductive because it somehow goaded her to seek more from him. He gave her whatever she seemed willing to take but nothing else.

Her lips rustled across his like a butterfly on a leaf and her fingertips moved to the breadth of his shoulders. She felt him catch his breath when her nails flexed momentarily into the material of his shirt.

123

"You make me feel like a rock being wrapped in silk," he murmured as his mouth obligingly found the delicate length of her neck.

Her fingers slid inside the collar of his shirt, searching out the warm skin underneath. She could have told him that she had never been able to make Drew feel like that, but she didn't know how to say the words, so Calla rained kisses across his cheek and down his throat. She let her mouth follow her fingers as she slowly unfastened the buttons of his shirt.

And when his hands at last went to the opening of her green shirt she sighed longingly, her eyes closed luxuriously as she savored the feel of his touch.

"I think your body must have been made for mine," he continued in a husky whisper. When she put out the tip of her tongue to touch the flat, masculine nipples, he curved his palm around her soft shape.

"I love the womanly strength in you, little one. Your breasts fill my hands like small, perfectly ripe fruit and they come alive at the tips when I touch you just so . . ."

He let his palm graze her nipples, sending shivers throughout her body and drawing a moan from her lips.

"See what I mean?" he whispered thickly. "And what about you, sweetheart, do you like the feel of me?"

She heard the soft demand in his words and couldn't deny it. Her hands slid through the rough pelt of hair on his chest and down to his waist as she leaned into him.

"You must know that I do," she said huskily, barely able to speak. "You know so much about me!"

"Do I?"

"Don't tease me, Slade!" she begged, her head curled beneath his chin as she explored his skin with circling fingertips.

"I wouldn't dream of it!" he vowed. "I've already told you that I'm yours . . . if you want me badly enough."

Under the impetus of her weight, he sank back into the corner of the couch and Calla sprawled lightly on top of him, thrilling unexpectedly to the sensation of dominance. She could make love to him as much as she liked and he would respond to her every touch, a small, gloating voice said in her mind.

Her kisses became more impassioned, and when he slid his hands under the green shirt and around her waist she shivered in delight. Her hips arched into his of their own accord, seeking the close, heated contact with unrestrained desire.

Deliberately she moved her jeaned legs along his, glorying in the groan of response deep in his chest. The one or two kisses she had planned to steal grew into heavy, drugging caresses as her mouth again sought his and her tongue slid inside.

She was slipping over an edge and a part of her knew it. The other part didn't seem to care. Just a little farther, it urged tantalizingly. What harm could there be? She could always bring things to a halt.

"Slade, oh, Slade! I've never felt quite like this before . . ."

"Isn't it time you asked yourself why it's different between us?" he suggested a little too softly.

"I don't know. I'm not sure I want to know!" she cried desperately, and stopped his mouth again with her own. She didn't want to talk about it. She only wanted to experience it. It seemed safer that way. Her brain was not ready to be coerced into the commitment her body was demanding.

Perhaps it was his question that finally triggered her rational mind into putting up some measure of protest. Perhaps it was only the cold, hard metal of his buckle pressing into the soft skin of her stomach. Calla couldn't be sure but she did realize finally that things were going much too far.

Drawing a great gulp of air, she raised her head and began to pull back, both physically and emotionally. She knew, even as he let her go at once, that she had been half-hoping, half-expecting him to cling to her, force her to stay and complete what she had started.

But four years of wariness and self-discipline made themselves felt with the rush of a falling theater curtain. Slowly, deliberately, Calla sat up and watched in silence as Slade lifted his arms and folded them behind his head. He remained reclining against the couch corner.

His golden brown eyes probed over her love-softened face and down her throat to her exposed breasts. Hastily, feeling the heat in her cheeks, Calla fumbled with the buttons of her shirt.

"Coward," he chided gently.

She turned away, unable to meet his look, and put out a shaking hand for the cognac snifter.

"You told me I could have as much as I wanted," she replied with an attempt at nonchalance. "I took what I wanted."

"Now you're a liar," he scoffed, but his voice was almost kind.

"How do you know?" she was driven to snap, aware of her hair hanging wantonly around her shoulders. "I told you I'm satisfied with what I got!"

"You don't know the meaning of the word," he retorted in a drawling rasp that flicked her nerves like a whip.

Her hand shook as she held the snifter to her lips. "I'm thirty years old, Slade. And these are emancipated times, in case you haven't heard. Women do know the meaning of satisfaction these days!" She gulped a bit too much of the cognac and felt it burn all the way down her throat.

126

And some women, she added silently, know the meaning of being able to satisfy a man about whom they care very much. . . .

"But not you," he said coolly. "Not yet."

"I have no intention of discussing the subject further. Isn't it about time you went home?" she said icily.

"Throwing me out on my ear, are you?" He sighed, sitting up and buttoning his shirt slowly. "A cruel, hard-hearted woman."

"Oh, Slade, I don't mean to throw you out," she relented immediately, turning pleading, uncertain eyes on him. "But this is as far as I mean things to go and I don't want . . ." She broke off and licked her lips. "I don't want you to think . . ."

"That you're a tease?" He grinned, ruffling her hair affectionately. "It's too late, sweetheart. I already think the worst of you!"

She winced. "I didn't mean . . ."

"Sure you did," he proclaimed, getting lithely to his feet and tucking his shirt back into the waistband of his slacks. "You meant to sample as much of me as you wanted tonight, regardless of how it left me feeling!"

Her eyes narrowed at the accusation. "Well, it's all your own fault! You're the one who said you didn't mind being teased!"

"I never said that. I merely said I'd put up with it, if that's all I could get." He leaned down and dropped a small kiss on her nose.

"Are you going home to a cold shower?" she taunted resentfully.

"No, I'm going home to a cold swim in my pool. Want to come along?"

"Good night, Slade," she said very firmly, getting to her feet and following him to the door.

"Good night, sweetheart. I'll see you at work tomorrow. Perhaps getting back to our routine style of fighting will be good for us!"

And, as usual, he was right, Calla had to admit. Slade was as good as his word about keeping their personal relationship out of the work situation, at least in front of others.

He arrived in her office Tuesday morning and was ushered in by a beaming secretary.

"Mr. York is here, Miss Nevin," Joyce said on a barely concealed note of excitement. A new boss was bound to be cause for curiosity, gossip, and anticipation.

"Thank you, Joyce," Calla said dryly, not bothering to point out that her secretary was stating the obvious. She smiled politely and with deliberate distance at Slade as he came forward and took a seat across from her.

"I'm having Lester's office cleaned and prepared for you so that you'll have a place to work from when you're visiting this branch of your business," she began formally, her hands folded calmly in front of her on the desk.

"That should work out fine," he smiled, every bit as politely as she had but perhaps not with such an implied distance. "I believe this was the morning I was due to meet the first-level supervisors?"

"Yes, if that's still agreeable with you?"

He nodded. "You said you wanted to discuss something with me first. Are you concerned about my announcing your appointment as manager of this end of the business in that memo this morning?"

"No," she said, brushing it aside. The ensuing flap had died down rather quickly. Perhaps the rest of the staff had guessed what was in the offing. Most of her peers had been happy for her. "I wanted to make certain you understood our experiment with Quality Circles before you met with the first-line supervisors. They're a crucial part of it and

128

they're very enthusiastic about the approach." She frowned slightly.

"But you're afraid it might not fit in with my management style?" he hazarded, mouth quirking slightly.

"You've got to admit, it might not fit in with your, uh, direct way of doing things!"

"I'm always open to new ideas, Miss Nevin," he informed her, amber eyes glinting. "Suppose you tell me exactly how far you've gone with the experiment."

"Quite a ways, I'm afraid. And it's met with such approval from every level of the staff that I don't want you to be hasty about disbanding it! You're familiar with the concept?"

"Quality Circles?" he smiled. "Of course. It's a Japanese style of management used to promote quality control. There's a great deal of interest in trying to implement it in American firms."

She nodded. "Then you know it's fairly simple, basically. Small groups of workers meet regularly with their supervisor to deal with quality problems and suggest ways of solving them. Everyone has an input, from the lowest level worker on up. Handled properly, it promotes enthusiasm and company loyalty. It gives every worker a feeling of making a direct contribution."

"I also know that several major Japanese executives have warned about the pitfalls of trying to simply imitate the Japanese methods. Differences in culture and background create different attitudes among workers. What works well in one culture doesn't necessarily work in another."

"The key is to take it very slowly, which we've done here at Chapman, Inc.—I mean, at your new branch of York Instruments," Calla amended swiftly. "It has to be a willing, voluntary thing and workers have to know their comments and suggestions are heeded."

"You don't think I'm capable of managing in that fashion?" he taunted lightly.

She sighed, rising gracefully to her feet. "We'll soon find out, won't we?" she retorted, leading the way toward the door.

In spite of her forebodings, however, Slade meshed very well with his new staff. He left absolutely no doubt about who was in command, but he also refrained from giving the impression he was going to trample through the ranks and reorganize everything at once. Calla could almost hear the sighs of relief among both management and workers as everyone realized that the transition would proceed smoothly.

He took her out to dinner on Tuesday night, tolerating afterward more of her tentative lovemaking until Calla once again lost her nerve and withdrew. As she watched him drive off into the night, she began to wonder who was doing the most suffering after the passionate interludes. Slade claimed he was going home to a swim or a cold shower but Calla found no easy way to get rid of the restlessness that seized her.

On Wednesday evening she fixed dinner for him, excelling herself with scampi and a Caesar salad. Slade seemed appreciative of her efforts and teased her about the cooking rivalry that threatened to develop.

"Worried about the threat to your ego?" she teased, and then wished she'd kept her mouth shut.

"Not in the least," he assured her with grand certainty. "Competition only improves the product in cases like this. The main thing to worry about is both of us getting fat!"

That night after he'd left, Calla stalked into the bedroom, pulled on her swimming suit, and tried his own remedy for dampening sexual desire. It wasn't all that effective, she decided, floating on her back in the quiet pool and gazing up at the brilliant desert night.

Oh, it cooled the unfamiliar fires flickering in her body, but nothing could squelch the images in her head.

And such images! Calla turned and dove for the bottom of the lighted pool. She held her breath, staring up at the night sky again and noticing how much different it looked from beneath five feet of chlorinated water.

When her breath ran out she bounded to the surface and as she broke through she admitted the truth. She was in love with the wretched man.

In love and scared to death.

Where did that leave her? Calla stroked for the pool edge, hauling herself up over the side with easy strength and snapping off the swimming cap with an absent gesture.

Whoever heard of being in love and scared to death at the same time?

She needed time. That was the problem, she told herself industriously as she reached for the striped towel. She needed time and somehow everything was happening much too fast.

There could be no better reason for going ahead with the trip to Tucson, she decided, walking back toward her condominium. A couple of days away from Slade would allow her to catch her breath and sort things out in her head. There were so many uncertainties.

Yes, she would go to Tucson and try to regain perspective. Perhaps this wasn't love. Perhaps what she felt was only the natural reaction of a woman who has experienced physical needs after four long years of isolation.

No, it wasn't that simple, she thought wryly as she changed into her nightgown. It was more than physical desire and she knew it. But the man was all wrong for her! Couldn't she get that through her head? How could she be contemplating marriage after only a few days . . .

No, it was after more than a month of knowing Slade,

131

she reminded herself. A month of coming to know him well on an intellectual level. And now she was learning him on a physical level. The combination was a potent one.

Yes, she needed the Tucson trip.

But Thursday night happened first.

132

Calla took the call from Slade late Thursday afternoon shortly before she was about to leave the office.

"Honey?" His voice was crisp and faintly annoyed. "I'm going to be held up here for a while. Probably a long while, so we're going to have to cancel the dinner plans. Does that break your heart?"

"I won't let myself starve, if that's what you're concerned about, but I will miss the lasagna you promised me!"

"The way to a woman's heart is through her stomach," he misquoted in satisfaction. "Think of me while you're opening a can of tuna fish."

"Just for that I'll manage something a little fancier than tuna! And I'll have a glass of wine to go with it."

"Going to ballet class this evening?" he asked in that suspiciously neutral tone she was coming to associate with impending disapproval.

"Of course!" The question surprised her. "Why?"

"Just wondering," he sighed. "You will remember what I told you about staying clear of Crispin, won't you?"

"Do you remember what I told you about not liking possessiveness in a man?" she retorted, evading the question.

"I remember, but we don't always get everything we want in life. Sometimes we have to make little compromises."

"Name one little compromise you've made so far," she invited dryly.

"If I were to start on my list, we'd never finish the

133

conversation in time for you to get to class. I will, however, mention one small item . . ." he began silkily.

"And what might that be?"

"The patience in which I have managed to possess myself for the past five weeks!"

"Patience!" she snapped, glad he couldn't see the rising heat in her cheeks. "Is that what you call it? I'd hate to see you impatient!"

"Keep that in mind when you're trying to tease me about Crispin," he recommended with feeling.

"I am not teasing you about Gary." The mild accusation stung her. "I was trying to make a point about possessiveness."

"I already know how you feel about it, but that's the way things are going to be between us so you might as well accept it. Now, sweetheart, I've got to get back to work. Stop trying to play cute with me and tell me you'll behave yourself this evening."

"I will behave myself this evening because I always behave myself!"

"I shall have to be satisfied with that, I suppose," he groaned.

"Yes," she agreed rashly, "you will."

"Courting you is like trying to crawl through a rose thicket. One wonders if one will ever get past the thorns and be able to collect flowers!"

"Think of the project as putting a little more balance in your life," she suggested kindly, stifling a chuckle.

"Are you feeling smug because your more 'focused' existence makes you stronger in situations like this? You think you can handle yourself and me, too?"

"I wouldn't dream of making such a provocative statement. At least, not out loud."

"Don't congratulate yourself yet," he advised smoothly. "Those of us who have a more balanced perspective are

134

much more capable of handling little shocks and adjustments. We can envision change. People like you who have set your course in one direction without looking either to the right or left are the ones who run afoul of unpredictable snags. When you come tumbling down you'll be the one who's most surprised. Me, I'll have been expecting it all along!"

"Do you always wax philosophical when you're forced to break a date and work late?"

"I try," he chuckled.

"Keep it up. It's probably good self-discipline!"

"I'm not the one who's such an advocate of self-discipline. You're the one who's built a life around it! Good-bye, honey. I'll call you at your office in the morning."

"Good-bye, Slade. Don't, uh, work too hard!" she taunted lightly and hung up the phone with a smile.

It was halfway through ballet class, when Calla was in the middle of a series of precisely executed battements, that she remembered Slade still hadn't mentioned the forthcoming Tucson trip. The jagged memory was enough to destroy her concentration. Although her extended leg seemed to return with a proper snap to fifth position, the eagle eye of Miss Marsden was on her as if the determined woman had read Calla's mind and knew it was wandering.

"You must raise the working leg much higher than that, Calla! These are battements à la hauteur, not à la demi-hauteur! Another ten, please."

Calla forced the thought of Slade out of her mind and summoned her full concentration.

The combined effort of having to work very hard at concentrating as well as the physical exertion left her exhausted, and Calla was not prepared to find Gary Crispin once again waiting for her to emerge from the dressing room. She was thinking only of getting home to a shower when she nearly collided with his solid form in the hall.

"I see your friend isn't waiting to pick you up tonight." He smiled obliquely, his dark eyes watching her intently. The black hair was casually ruffled with that Byronic air that probably had made him very attractive onstage.

"I guess he thought I could make it home alone," she heard herself say with a touch of impatience, and immediately felt apologetic. She covered the retort with a polite smile. "And home is exactly where I'm headed. Miss Marsden was in fine form this evening!"

"She's always in fine form," Gary remarked dismissingly. "Fortunately for me York isn't going to be able to run off with her as easily as he appears to have run off with you!"

"Gary!" Calla stared at him, startled. The hand she had been using to wield a towel around her damp neck and shoulders stilled. "What a thing to say!"

"Oh, he made himself very clear the other evening when he picked you up after class." Gary smiled wryly, leaning against the wall with a studied pose that was probably more automatic than affected. Gary had been dancing a long time.

Calla frowned. "Was Slade rude to you?" she demanded, eyes narrowing.

"Not at all. He simply took one look at me, figured out who I was, and announced quite casually he was going to be marrying you soon. The implication was very clear. I was to stay out of the picture!"

Calla groaned. "Sometimes he's a bit blunt. And he thinks his plans are all cut and dried!"

"He's *not* going to marry you?" One black brow lifted interrogatingly.

"Oh, he's asked me, all right. But I haven't even begun to make up my mind." She smiled ruefully. "We've only known each other a little over a month and he's not really the kind of man . . ."

She let the sentence trail off, horrified at having voiced aloud the whirling thoughts that had been coursing through her mind all day. Gary was a friend, but there were some things one didn't discuss even with friends! At least, Calla didn't.

"It's okay, Calla," Gary soothed gently. "I don't mind listening. If you want to talk about it . . ."

Calla glanced hesitatingly up into the friendly dark eyes and tried to see if there was more than just friendliness there. For a moment she seriously considered telling Gary the whole story after all. It had been a long time since she'd enjoyed the relief of confiding in another human being. The temptation was strong. She drew a deep breath.

"Thanks, Gary. I appreciate the offer. But right now all I can think about is getting home to a shower!" She kept her voice light, joking. "And you certainly don't need a student crying on your shoulder just before you take on your advanced class!"

"Well . . ." He smiled bleakly, straightening from the wall. "The offer stands. If you ever need to talk about it, let me know."

"It's very kind of you . . ." But she knew she wouldn't and now he knew it too. Whatever might have been between them would never be allowed a chance to grow. Calla knew it was for the best. She could never have loved Gary. They would remain friends.

"Not at all. We can't have anything interfering with your concentration during class!" he teased, taking his cue and walking away.

Calla watched him go and tried to sort out the impressions he had left behind. For the first time she acknowledged that Slade's warning might have had some merit. Then she shook her head. It was no good. She was starting to view matters from Slade's possessive perspective. And possessiveness was a stupid, unreasoning, and immature emotion.

She had told Slade she and Gary were friends. That ought to be sufficient. He'd even told her he believed her, for heaven's sake! Calla guided the little green Fiat down an avenue lined with palms, aware of the fading heat of the desert evening.

It didn't make any sense, Calla thought grimly as she drove with idle attention. If Slade believed her about the relationship with Gary, why was he still possessive regarding the matter? At least it was a far cry from her ex-husband's reaction to the least hint of a friendship. Drew not only would never have believed her, he would have sulked and raged until she'd quit ballet.

Drew's irrational dislike of any of her friends hadn't been limited to the males in the crowd. It had applied to anyone who enjoyed Calla's company. It wasn't just her career that had suffered while she had been married to Drew. Her entire social life had ground to a halt.

God! She had been a fool to try to make that marriage work. She had stayed with Drew long enough to let him affect her whole life. Slade had been right about that. Drew had destroyed her confidence in herself as a woman, made her doubt her own ability in the business world, and then blamed her for the failure of the marriage.

If the truth be known, Calla thought, her hand clenching around the steering wheel, the marriage had been wrong from the start. Never again would she mistake romantic possessiveness and jealousy for true love! It was a sign of immaturity and childish arrogance in a man.

But how closely did Slade's possessiveness resemble Drew's? she asked herself later as she puttered around the kitchen, pouring the promised glass of wine and heating up a cheese and sprout sandwich.

Could she trust Slade to be as sure of himself as he

138

claimed? Or was he only so confident because he was her boss? And what about his reaction to Gary? Did that signal a hint of the irrational jealousy she'd experienced so painfully from Drew?

At least, Calla thought with a quirking smile, she was learning she still had some ability as a woman. There could be no doubt that Slade reacted to her physically. He wanted her very badly and she loved to hear his groans of desire, to feel the tautness of his body at her touch. . . .

She sipped her wine and forced herself to pursue the matter in her mind. Slade was aroused by her, that much was indisputable. But would he be satisfied with her? Drew had made it very clear she was a disappointment in bed. The affair with his secretary, she'd learned later, had begun shortly after the wedding.

The problem, naturally, she thought with a sigh, was that there was only one way to test the issue! And that one way carried very grave risks to her peace of mind.

Because going to bed with Slade York would be a commitment beyond anything she'd experienced before. Certainly beyond what she'd known in her marriage. And what happened to a woman who found her body and soul committed to a man if he didn't return that depth of feeling?

And no man could return the feeling if he wasn't passionately aroused and satisfied by a woman, could he?

Calla chewed thoughtfully on her lower lip as she rinsed her dishes in the sink. If she managed to satisfy Slade, would he cease to be possessive? Would he realize she couldn't possibly give herself like that to another man? Would he be able to fully trust her?

Her next marriage had to be founded on trust and love, Calla swore as she walked back into the living room. The thought stopped her for a minute and she smiled wryly.

A couple of weeks ago she would have said that in all likelihood there would never be a "next marriage." Now here she was trying to define the terms under which it would exist!

After four long years of control and concentrated drive in an unerring direction, it was a shock to think of veering even slightly from her course.

Calla picked up a book on achieving one's goals through self-discipline and organization and forced herself to read for a time, but the restlessness that had pervaded her mind whenever she was not occupied with work or dancing this week returned.

After a few chapters, she put down the self-help guide and got to her feet. It was quite dark outside now. She peered out across her patio to the dimly lit pool area and decided on an impulse to take a swim. The water would still be comfortably warm from the day's heat and perhaps it would relax her before she tried to sleep.

She slipped into the sleek maillot, grabbed a towel, and walked through the patio and across the lawn to the underwater-lit pool.

The water was everything she'd hoped it would be. Somehow, gliding through the silent liquid restored a sense of tranquillity and perspective. She had the place to herself at this late hour and it was pleasant to float on the surface and gaze at the heavens.

She was in love. Why did everything always have to come back to that? How could she even know what it meant after the disaster of her marriage? But something in her knew. Something deep and primitive and female. Slade was different. But was he different enough to allow her to risk marriage?

Cleaving the water with a silent surface dive, she sank to the bottom, rolling over and holding her breath while she watched the dark sky through several feet of water.

Something moved, casting a long shadow on the disturbed surface, and Calla let the rest of her breath escape. Perhaps another condominium owner had opted for a late-night swim. Slowly, languidly, she rose to the surface, her head turning to face the shadow.

"Slade!"

He stood beside the pool, still dressed in his suit and tie, the coat slung over one shoulder and caught by a careless hand. He was watching her intently, the amber eyes gleaming down at her as she treaded water.

"I couldn't stay away," he said simply.

She felt the electricity in the air and swallowed carefully. "Did you get through all your business?"

"Yes."

"You look exhausted."

"I am."

She smiled with a sudden sense of impishness. "Why don't you join me?"

He cocked an eyebrow. "The neighbors don't mind nude swimming?"

"Leave your shorts on. They cover more than that excuse for a bathing suit you wore last weekend!" she retorted, chuckling.

"Spoilsport."

But his fingers went to his tie and in a surprisingly short time he had stripped down to his white Jockey shorts. Calla glanced hurriedly away.

"I don't think I'll risk a dive." He grinned, sliding into the water from the pool edge. "I wouldn't want to shock your sensitivities by emerging without the shorts."

She stood back, her hands passing idly in arcs through the water, as she watched him stroke powerfully from one end of the pool to the other. She could watch him forever, she thought suddenly, and dove to cool off her burning face.

141

When she came up again he was nearby, waiting for her.

"Feel better?" she asked lightly, supremely aware of the excitement in just being near him tonight.

"Much."

"You're not very chatty this evening," she teased, maintaining the distance under the heat of his eyes.

"No."

"Did the work that kept you late concern that bid proposal for the airplane instrumentation contract you mentioned a few days ago?"

"Umm."

"Stop me if I'm boring you." She grinned.

"You're not. You never bore me."

She studied his enigmatic expression in the exotic light reflecting up through the blue-green water.

"Maybe you're still not relaxed," she suggested softly.

"Perhaps."

"Float on your back," she ordered, gliding forward. "I'll hold you."

Obediently he leaned backward, making no effort to keep himself afloat with his hands. She slipped her palms under his back, maintaining his weight easily with the assistance of the buoyant water.

"How's that?" She began sliding her feet along the bottom of the pool, pulling him through the water and enjoying the feel of him.

"Terrific," Slade murmured, closing the dark coffee lashes and giving himself up entirely to the sensation.

Calla liked that. There was a curious sense of power in floating him through the water. It gave her a feeling of both protecting and comforting him. A nice, womanly feeling. The sort of womanly power a water goddess might have over a tired water god.

Smiling at her own fantasy, she moved him back and forth through the water, watching him to her heart's content. The fine, smoothly muscled body seemed quite content to let her take the lead. The tanned chest gleamed wetly and the dark hair glistened on his forehead.

She felt her confidence brimming over as she guided his progress. His body trusted hers, she thought abstractedly. He trusted her. He was willing to let her assume control. After that alarming assault the night of the party at the country club he had never again pushed her physically.

She hummed unconsciously as she moved.

"You're very good at sweeping me off my feet and carrying me away," he whispered after a time. "You should do it more often!"

Calla pulled her hands out from under his back and watched him sink. She was laughing when he sputtered to the surface an instant later.

"Unkind!" he complained, turning reproachful eyes on her as he flipped the water out of his way.

"You should learn to keep your mouth shut when things are going well for you," she advised with a smile. "Did you ever get dinner tonight?"

"I had a sandwich around six. About the time you were getting out of your ballet class."

"Hungry?"

"Starved. Got any leftover tuna fish?"

"No, and if I did, I wouldn't admit it. I do have some cheese and crackers you can snack on, if you like."

"I like." He watched her swim toward the edge of the pool. "Did you see Crispin after class?"

She turned, in the act of hauling herself out of the water, and paused, frowning.

"Yes."

"Did he ask you out?"

She finished hauling herself over the side. "No." That much was the truth, if not all the truth.

143

"He will," Slade predicted, extending sinewy arms over the edge to follow her out of the pool.

She shrugged, turning away to fetch the towel. "So?"

"So it will be easier on everyone concerned if you let him know where he stands now before it gets to that point."

"It's my business, Slade," she said coolly, rubbing herself briskly and freeing her hair from the cap. She handed him the towel without looking at him.

"That's a ridiculous statement and you know it, little one," he said gently.

"You'll just have to trust me, won't you?" she said with far too much sweetness in her voice.

"It's got nothing to do with trust. I'm trying to protect you from a potentially awkward situation. I want him to bury any ideas he's getting about you."

She watched as he toweled the coffee-dark hair, her head tipped to one side speculatively. "I gather you've already tried to set him straight on the subject!"

Slade quirked his mouth wryly. "He told you about our little conversation?"

"And then offered to let me confide in him if I felt the need of a *friend.*"

"And you believed him?" There was cool mockery in the gritty rough voice.

"You really can't conceive of a friendship between a man and a woman, can you?" she murmured sadly, watching as he wrapped the towel around his waist and picked up his clothing.

"I think the kind of friendship Crispin wants is very dangerous. I don't want you to put yourself in a difficult situation."

"At least you try to argue rationally about it," Calla suddenly teased, leading the way back across the lawn to her home.

144

"That doesn't imply I feel rationally about it," he retorted, chuckling.

"Just using the approach you think might work best?"

"Probably."

"I'll make you a deal. Don't mention Gary again this evening and I'll fix you a plate of cheese and crackers while you're showering!"

"You always do drive a hard bargain," he sighed. But he let the subject go with surprising alacrity.

Calla spent a quick few minutes under the hot shower and slipped into a housecoat and scuffs, brushing out her hair and letting it hang softly around her shoulders. In the mirror her blue-green eyes gleamed like the sea.

"All yours," she said easily, coming back into the living room, where he still waited wrapped in the towel. He'd pulled his glasses out of his jacket pocket and was thumbing through the book on building self-discipline that she had been reading earlier. He was standing.

"Thanks," he said, glancing up and removing the glasses absently. "I don't suppose you have a robe to lend me, too?"

"Sorry, I haven't made elaborate arrangements for entertaining visiting males," she drawled. "I can put the shorts in the dryer for you while you're in the shower. The waistband might stay damp but otherwise they should be okay."

The golden-brown eyes glittered for a moment but all he said was "I'm glad you're not overly prepared for men in your home."

He threw the jockey shorts out into the hall after he'd disappeared into the bathroom and Calla tossed them into the dryer, setting the heat as high as possible. When he called for them fifteen minutes later they were reasonably dry. She handed them into him along with a snifter of the good cognac.

"You know how to make a man comfortable," he murmured from the other side of the door, accepting both.

Calla smiled, experiencing a very pleasant feeling at the intimate situation. It was almost homey, in a manner she'd forgotten or perhaps never really had a chance to know well. A nice feeling. Good Lord! Had she been lonely for the past four years and not even realized it?

When he wandered out into the living room wearing the gray slacks of his suit and his shirt, unbuttoned, she was waiting, curled into a corner of the couch.

"An excellent idea, going for a swim," he applauded softly, sinking languidly down beside her and reaching for the crackers and cheese.

"How did you know where to come looking for me?" she asked idly, enjoying his wolfish appetite.

His fingers conveying the last bite to his mouth froze for a second. And then he smiled bleakly. "Your car was in the parking lot. I figured you had to be around somewhere. It was a logical choice to check the pool."

"Logical? You mean after you'd dismissed the idea I might have been out with Gary Crispin?" she hazarded with unbidden perception.

"It was your idea not to bring him up again this evening," he reminded her gently, not looking at her.

"Was that one of the things contributing to the exhausted look I saw on your face when you found me in the pool? You were afraid I was with Gary?" For the life of her, Calla didn't know why she was pressing the issue.

"This cheddar is excellent. Where did you get it?"

"Slade . . ."

"I'd rather not discuss my look of exhaustion. Not good for my ego. A man should be able to take a few late hours at work without showing the ill effects. I don't want to contemplate the idea that I might be losing some of my youthful vigor," he joked.

146

But when the amber eyes met hers she knew.

"Oh, Slade. Can't you trust me?" she whispered beseechingly.

"You haven't gone out of your way to reassure me," he said mildly. "But, yes, I trust you. You don't understand, that's all. And I honestly don't know how to explain it."

"Possessiveness?"

"All I can say is that until you experience it yourself, you'll just have to take my word that it exists and that it's part of a relationship like ours."

"Well, at least you're not yelling at me about it," she tried to say on a light note.

"Only because I know it wouldn't do any good," he groaned, leaning back against the couch as he polished off the last of the cheddar.

"Believe it or not I consider that a step in the right direction," she whispered, blue-green eyes glowing softly.

"Do you?"

"Yes."

The tension ebbed and flowed around them as their eyes met, and then Slade set down his snifter with great exactness.

"I think," he stated flatly, starting to get to his feet, "that I'd better be on my way. It's getting late."

Calla uncurled and stood beside him, aware of that feeling of hovering on a brink. An uncomfortable feeling, fraught with alertness, wariness, tension, and uncertainty. She had known it far too often around Slade York and this past week had given her moments that had made her want to scream.

She knew as she stood there looking up at him that ever since he had appeared by the pool she had been looking forward to the moment when he would let her initiate the gentle lovemaking. And now he was leaving without even a kiss.

147

And she didn't want him to go. Not tonight. Not ever. But some of the self-confidence she had been gaining receded as he stood waiting for the flickering emotions in her eyes to come to a conclusion.

He knew what she was thinking, Calla realized. He didn't move. He simply waited for her to make up her mind. The responsibility was all hers.

But she barely knew him, a last, fading voice in her head protested. Only a week . . .

No, that wasn't true. She had known him on another level for a month before this new aspect of their relationship had been allowed to intrude.

And what, after all, did time have to do with it? She had known Drew for much longer than that and still made the mistake of marrying him. This man wasn't Drew. She repeated that several times in her head with a wondering sensation. There was still the possessiveness and there was the way he had tried to force himself on her last Friday night . . .

But he hadn't forced himself on her, not in the final analysis. He had been frustrated but he'd behaved in a civilized fashion even if it had been a high-handed one.

The possessiveness? Well, it would seem he was learning to handle that, too. He hadn't yelled at her about it lately. He hadn't sulked or accused. He'd simply tried to state his case.

"Slade," Calla said in a soft, aching whisper, her eyes glowing with the fire beneath the seas. "Please don't go."

His mouth twisted slightly and the amber eyes warmed. He put out a hand and touched her loosened hair. "I don't think I'm strong enough to take the teasing tonight, little one. As you noted, I've had a rough day. Tonight I've enjoyed the relaxing in the pool and using your shower and eating the snack you prepared. But I think that's about as far as I'd better let things go. You look much too inviting in your cozy robe and slippers."

Calla caught her breath, putting up a hand to cradle the one in her hair. She turned her face into it the way a cat turns into the stroke of its master's hand.

"I am feeling inviting, too," she said in such a low voice he barely heard her.

She felt his fingers close convulsively around hers and didn't dare meet his eyes.

"Is tonight the night, my sweet Calla?" he rasped whimsically. "Are you going to carry me off to your bed and love me the way I've been longing to have you love me?"

Calla felt another brief surge of uncertainty. What if she wasn't capable of giving him the kind of love he sought? But her own needs and her blossoming love for this man would no longer heed the warning.

Without another word she took the hand she held and started down the hall, leading Slade off to her waiting bed.

CHAPTER NINE

He followed her without a word, his hand wrapped secure-ly around hers. Calla felt the trembling in his lean, hard body when she stopped in the bedroom doorway and turned into his arms with a small sigh. She buried her face against the material of his shirt, shivering with longing and a strange kind of anxiety.

"Calla, my sweet," he whispered into her hair as his hands gentled her spine, "are you sure?"

Her voice was steady although barely audible. "I'm sure, Slade." Then she remembered what he needed to hear from her.

"I want you, Slade. I want you so badly that nothing else matters anymore. I need you!"

"I've told you before," he rasped thickly, "I'm all yours. I have been since the first day I saw you. I would have let you carry me off right then and there if you'd shown any sign of being willing!"

She could sense his smile and knew the amber eyes were heating with warmth and soft humor. Her own lips curved in a small smile as she nuzzled past the opening of his shirt and kissed the skin of his chest.

"Instead you decided to play hard to get," she teased, the tip of her tongue reaching out to taste him.

"I suggest we don't argue about who was playing hard to get. Not tonight," he pleaded with the urgency of a man who is so close to his heart's desire that he doesn't want anything to get in the way.

"Oh, Slade!"

She wrapped her arms around his neck in a circle of love and fire that brought her body tight against his. Lifting her face invitingly, she met his lowered mouth with the hunger and need that had been building in her since the first time he'd kissed her.

Perhaps, she thought vaguely, perhaps it had been building before that time. Perhaps it had stirred to life during the month of intense intellectual battle. It didn't matter any longer. Now, tonight, was the only reality. The only time that counted.

Eagerly, with the confidence and audacity she had been learning in his arms during the strange courtship, Calla parted her lips. She dared the tip of her tongue past his teeth, seeking the small duel she would find there.

His mouth opened to receive her and she gloried in the exchange of warmth and the promise of passion. His groan of response excited and thrilled her.

Unconsciously she rose to balance on her toes, using the dancer's strength to give herself more height and more access to the tantalizing areas of his throat and ear.

"My God, Calla! I want you so badly it hurts."

Slade's hands on her back slid farther to the curve of her hips and beyond, his fingers clenching with desire and leaping passion. Calla shut her sea-colored eyes against the rapture of knowing he wanted her as much as she wanted him. This was right. This was the way it should be. The way it had never been . . .

And then she thrust all thought of the past out of her mind and concentrated on finding all the ways to please the man she loved.

Her fingers curled into the rich darkness of his still-damp hair and she inhaled the clean male scent of him. All of her senses seemed to become involved in the lovemaking, each seeking to satisfy itself in its own way.

Slade's hands went to the belt of her housecoat as Calla inserted her fingers under the collar of his shirt. When she pushed it off the broad, tanned shoulders, he followed suit.

She felt the housecoat gliding to the floor to settle in a pool at her feet and smiled intimately to herself. He was once again letting her set the pace.

"I'm still in charge, I see." She laughed lovingly up at him from under her lashes as her nails lightly scored his shoulders.

"Why not? You do such an excellent job of seducing me!" The gold in his eyes almost burned her.

Calla felt something very female inside herself stir to flaming life at the implication. She could give this man what he wanted. She could please him!

Her sense of sureness grew by leaps and bounds as her hands went to the metal buckle of his belt. Her fingers were trembling, but from eagerness, not fear.

"So sweet and strong and lovely," Slade groaned a moment later as they both stood naked, drinking in the sight of each other's bodies. "A body to match your mind."

Calla swept her hands down his rib cage to his lean, narrow hips, relishing the hard, uncompromising maleness of him and then pressed herself close.

"Let me love you, Slade," she begged seductively.

"What do you think I've been waiting for these past few weeks?"

But he made no move to assert himself, although there could be no doubt about his arousal. For every caress Calla gave him, she received one just as warm and hungry in return. But he didn't play the male role she had half-expected him to assume when matters had reached such a point. She was to bear the responsibility for what happened tonight.

And suddenly Calla realized she was going to glory in her power. Feeling like the goddess she had imagined herself to be earlier in the swimming pool, she stepped back and tugged Slade over to the bed.

He went down beneath her impulsive little shove, pull-

153

ing her sprawling on top of him as he fell to the bed. She saw the delighted anticipation on his face and smiled boldly from her dominant position on top of his chest.

"I think I've created a little wildcat," he grinned devilishly, his hands ruffling through the floating bronze of her hair. "Did you know you had the makings of such a brazen hussy?"

"No, Mr. York," she drawled invitingly, bending to drop a tiny kiss beneath his chin. The roughness of his incipient beard scraped her slightly. "Just one of the many things I'm discovering under the tutelage of my new boss."

"I believe you did mention at one point that you're always ready to learn . . ."

"You're going to take full credit for the transformation?"

"Shouldn't I?" he mocked, his hands seeking her small, firm breasts.

"No, I don't think so," she decided judiciously between little fiery kisses down his throat. "I think the ability must have always been there inside me. I've just never had the opportunity of using it before!"

"Are you telling me I'm a guinea pig?"

"Do you feel like a guinea pig?" she countered, laughing huskily.

"No," he admitted thickly. "I feel like a man who's found himself in bed with a full-blooded woman."

Breathlessly she moved on his body, exploring, learning, indulging her deepest instincts to please and to find pleasure in return. And with every new adventure, there was a corresponding, uninhibited response from Slade that drove her on to another discovery.

When her leg moved against his she felt the tremor in him and delighted in it. When she took a tiny, convulsive nip from his shoulder he groaned and she felt his nails sinking into the flesh of her buttocks. The small pain seemed to send her into a frenzy of desire and she clung to him, arching herself into his heat with open longing.

"You make me lose my head, do you know that? I feel half crazy when you're this close . . ." Slade used his own teeth gently on her nipple.

"Only half?" she teased on a note of urgent passion.

"You don't care if you push me over the edge?" he asked warningly.

But Calla was past paying any heed to a man's warnings tonight. She only knew something was driving her to find the limits for both of them. It had become the most important goal in her life and she applied herself to it with all the strength of will she had been developing for four long years.

The heat and power they were generating seemed to fill the room, locking them in a silken cocoon of passion unlike anything Calla had ever experienced. She twisted eagerly, enticingly against Slade, urging his body to respond to hers and thrilling to the knowledge that he needed very little incentive.

His fingers circled the tips of her breasts, drawing a shudder from her body that seemed to please him. She responded with a wet, moist caress near his ear, and her hands cradled his head for another deep, probing kiss of his mouth.

"I don't think I can wait any longer for you, my sweet Calla," he grated hoarsely. "Put me out of my agony!"

It was a command and a plea and Calla reacted to it with an instinctive desire to goad and to provoke.

"You didn't say please," she taunted softly, her hair sweeping across his chest as she trailed her fingers down his flat, hard stomach and beyond.

"Is that what you want?" he demanded on a harsh gasp

155

as she feathered the inside of his thigh. "Do you want me to plead for you to finish what you've started?"

"I think it might be interesting to hear you beg," she told him wickedly, knowing that if he didn't, she wouldn't be able to hold out much longer anyway. God! How she wanted him! Loved him. Needed him. . . .

"You *are* a tease, aren't you?" he growled fiercely. "I should have known what would happen when I set out to let you find your own power!"

"You mean you didn't expect to find yourself begging for me?" she murmured on a note of provocative amusement.

"No," he grated. "I only wanted you to find out what you could do to me and yourself. But I think I outdid myself."

He moved suddenly, unexpectedly. Calla felt his lean, strong body shift beneath her, felt his hands seize her waist and lift her away from him.

"No!" she cried, terribly afraid that she had gone too far and had angered him. He was going to push her aside and leave. . . .

Desperately she clutched at his arms. "Please, Slade, don't leave me!"

"What made you think I was going anywhere?" he smiled with sexy menace as he settled her flat on her back against the bedclothes and lowered himself to cover the length of her writhing body. "I'm only going to show you what happens to bold women who don't know when to stop teasing. . . ."

Wide-eyed she stared up at him in wonder and comprehension for an instant, analyzing the amber flames beneath the coffee-colored lashes. Slowly, lovingly her arms twisted around his neck, pulling him down to her.

"I think," he muttered against her mouth, "that it's

156

time you learned there are a few male prerogatives left in this world!"

Calla opened her mouth to receive his exploring tongue just as he used his hips to crush her deeply into the bed. She gasped, responding to the overwhelming intimacy of the contact, and arched her body into his.

His knee pushed insistently at her legs until she shifted them willingly to allow him closer to her warmth.

"Slade!"

His name was a sudden, tight cry torn from her lips as he completed the union with erotic power and a driving grace that sent shudders through every region of her body.

Her nails bit deeply into his shoulders, drawing a sound of aggression and desire from him. He moved on her body, lowering a hand beneath her hips and compelling her to match his rhythm.

Calla felt her senses whirl into a never-ending spiral that left her helpless in the grip of a storm. She surrendered to it and at the same time clung to the man who had generated it as if to chain him there with her.

But even as she clutched at him, Calla knew somehow that Slade needed no further encouragement to stay. He was as lost in the whirling chaos of passion as she herself. She had dragged him over the edge with her as she stepped into the yawning pit that had been waiting for her ever since she'd met this man.

The knowledge of the true depths of her own female power excited and exulted. She gave with every ounce of her strength and love and took just as much in return.

The crescendo rose for both of them, awesome and intriguing beyond anything Calla had ever known. Her body recognized the impending explosion even though it had never experienced anything like it before. Her nerves tautened and her muscles shivered with tension.

"Yes! Oh, Slade, I can't stand it!" she gasped, her head

thrown back in primitive abandon as she clung to him. Something inside her must surely burst before this was over!

And it did when Slade seemed to gather himself for a final, dazzling display of male power. A power that could only be fully released by the female of the species, as she took it into herself and made it a part of her.

"Calla!" He shouted her name deep into her throat as she went momentarily rigid beneath him, her eyes squeezed tightly shut against the ultimate surge of passion.

Then he moved quickly against her once more, holding her shivering body tightly beneath him, as he found his own satisfaction in a hard, fierce final encounter.

He held her that way through the long descent back into the real world and Calla was aware of being wrapped in strength as she slowly regained her normal breathing pattern.

There was a dampness on their skins and an air of released sexual tension in the room. A musky scent filled her nostrils and she listened to his own recovering breath with tingling pleasure.

Slade stroked a hand through her tangled hair as she turned her face into his chest, nuzzling him like a cat.

For a long time neither spoke. By mutual consent they simply lay close together, enjoying the aftermath of the warmth they had created and shared.

Eventually Calla moved gently in Slade's embrace, raising her chin just enough to allow her eyes to meet his. The golden-brown depths gleamed down at her and she smiled back with lazy satisfaction and pleasure.

"Feeling quite pleased with yourself, Calla Nevin?" he chuckled richly, his hand wrapping itself more thoroughly in her hair, his eyes gazing at her from beneath half-lowered lids.

She stretched like a cat in his arms and sighed content-edly. "I don't hear you complaining," she mocked smugly.

He gave her a small, humorous shake. "Don't you dare take the full credit for what happened here tonight! I've been working for days on this!"

"And you'd still be working on it if I hadn't put you out of your misery tonight," she retorted sweetly, toying with the crisp hair of his chest.

"Hah! Is that all the thanks I'm going to get for letting you prove to yourself that you're a very healthy, very passionate young woman?" he murmured reproachfully.

She went very still in his arms.

"What is that supposed to mean?" Calla finally snapped, not knowing whether to be indulgent or angry at the male satisfaction in his voice.

He grinned with arrogant complacency. "Don't you think I knew almost from the beginning what the problem was?"

"You're going to congratulate yourself on unfreezing me, so to speak?" she asked in a neutral tone that at another time might have reminded Calla of him.

"Oh, no," he assured her with soft laughter. "You did all the work. I merely offered myself as the guinea pig, remember?"

"Guinea pigs are a dime a dozen," she tossed back loftily.

"But you needed a very special kind of guinea pig," he countered knowingly.

"What kind?" Calla's eyes narrowed suspiciously.

"The kind you could want badly enough to seduce. One who was willing to let you take your time and practice first before you went ahead with the full experiment."

"Are all men this arrogant after such a successful 'experiment'?"

"Beats me. I've never had such a degree of success before!"

"Slade?"

"Umm?"

"Shut up and let me experiment again."

"Yes, dear."

"You know the scientific method demands that an experiment be duplicated several times before it's fully accepted by the scientific community."

"There's nothing like a woman with a good education," he noted admiringly.

Calla reached up and pulled his head down to hers, trapping one of his thighs beneath her own.

It was very late when Slade eventually heaved himself to a sitting position on the edge of her bed and sat looking down at her for a long moment before getting to his feet.

"Slade?" Calla mumbled sleepily, putting out a hand to catch hold of him. "Where are you going?"

"Home, little one. We both have to be at work in the morning, remember? And I can't very well leave from here and arrive looking unshaven and rumpled, can I? I've got to go home and get dressed."

"It's almost daylight," she said half protestingly.

"I know. Go back to sleep, sweetheart. I'll call you at your office."

"I wish you didn't have to go. . . ."

"Do you?"

Calla tried briefly to understand what lay beneath the sudden advent of his neutral tone and then shrugged off the problem. It must be her imagination.

"Slade?"

"Yes, honey?" he asked. In the darkened room she could see him stepping into his slacks and clasping the belt.

160

"Drive carefully." It was all she could find to say. It was awkward, she was discovering, having one's lover leave before daylight. She levered herself up on her elbow, her hair fall onto her slightly raised shoulder and her blue-green eyes gleaming softly.

His mouth curved briefly as he pulled on his shirt. "I will," he promised before stepping close to the bed and leaning down to drop a kiss on her soft, slightly bruised mouth.

"I'll talk to you in the morning, Calla."

A few minutes later she heard the Mercedes purr to life out in the parking lot and then all was silent.

With a sigh Calla flopped back down against the pillows. She was wide awake now as she gazed out the window and watched the slowly lightening sky. Soon she wouldn't have to watch Slade leave in the early hours of the morning. She was going to marry him.

Yes, she would marry him, Calla told herself again, her eyes dreamy as she gazed toward the purpling mountains in the distance. She loved him and tonight she had proven she could satisfy him.

She smiled blissfully to herself. Slade was under the impression she had discovered that she was not a frigid woman. But that concern hadn't been nearly as important in her mind as her fear of failing to satisfy him. Well, let him think what he liked. It was probably good for his ego!

Not that his ego needed any special vitamins, she thought ruefully. How much of a problem was it going to be? Nothing she couldn't handle, she decided with a new sureness. Slade was not another Drew Sheridan. Every instinct told her that. Slade's ego was based on a healthy appreciation of his own abilities rather than a falsely inflated inner vision of himself. He could allow a woman to be successful without finding it a threat. He could even allow a woman to take the lead in lovemaking as he had

161

during the past few days. It went without saying that Drew would have been totally unable to tolerate a woman taking the initiative.

Calla shook her head, determined not to think about Drew ever again. Her whole attention from now on would be on Slade York. Drew simply wasn't important any longer.

Of course, there were one or two matters still to be worked out between herself and Slade, Calla reminded herself later that morning as she showered and dressed for work. He must be made to understand that there was no need to be possessive or jealous. One couldn't blame him, perhaps, for feeling that way after what he'd been through with his first wife, Calla admitted understandingly, but her relationship with him would be vastly different.

Love and understanding and trust. Those were the fundamental building bricks of a good marriage. She nodded to herself in the mirror as she thrust a last pin into the neat knot at the nape of her neck.

It was as she slipped behind the wheel of the Fiat that Calla made her decision. Why should she postpone telling Slade any longer? She would stop by his office on the way to work and let him know she'd made her decision. She would marry him.

She tried to picture his pleased expression and grinned to herself. There would probably be another bout of him congratulating himself on the success of his courtship! Well, she could allow him that much. After all, he had been successful!

As she parked the Fiat in the company lot and made her way toward the downtown offices of York Instruments, Calla asked herself how she could not have recognized the loneliness of the past four years.

But perhaps she hadn't really been lonely, she thought

162

in surprise as she walked crisply up the walk, her low-heeled pumps clicking brightly on the flagstones.

She had, after all, spent the last four years finding out a lot about herself. She had been busy building her own inner strength and forging a career. There had been plenty to occupy her mentally and physically while she deliberately took charge of her life. No, she couldn't truly describe the last four years as lonely. They had been a time of learning and growing.

Perhaps that learning and growing had been in a rather narrow area, though, she was willing to admit as she pushed open the swinging doors into the modern office building. Objectively speaking she could see she lacked some of the balance Slade had said was so important to his own life.

But everyone came to terms with herself or himself in his or her own way and Calla was satisfied with what she'd accomplished in the time since her divorce. She was ready now for marriage. A marriage of true equality.

She smiled brilliantly at the secretary guarding the entrance to Slade's suite of offices. The middle-aged woman smiled back in pleased recognition.

"Miss Nevin! Was Mr. York expecting you?" Mrs. Cosgrove glanced anxiously at her calendar.

"No, and it will probably serve me right if he's tied up right now and can't see me." Calla grinned. "I stopped by on the way to work on the off chance he might be free."

"I believe he's got a few minutes before his Friday morning management meeting. I'll let him know you're here."

Mrs. Cosgrove bent her graying head and spoke politely into the intercom on her desk.

"Miss Nevin is here, Mr. York. She would like to see you if you have a few minutes."

There was a slight pause from the instrument and then Slade's voice came, sounding calm and businesslike.

"Send her in, Mrs. Cosgrove."

With a nod, Mrs. Cosgrove indicated the inner door and Calla stepped forward. For an instant as she stood there, her hand poised on the knob, she felt a last flicker of uncertainty at what she was about to do.

But then she remembered Slade's clear pleasure and satisfaction last night. Of course he must still want to marry her!

She pushed open the door and closed it quickly behind her, blue-green eyes sweeping the tastefully furnished office with its mahogany desk and sweeping view of the city. From one window she could see Camelback Mountain, a local landmark.

Slade rose as she walked gracefully into the room, his amber eyes absorbing the crisp, professional look of her in the trim little suit and pumps. An emerald green scarf added a dash of color to the off-white suit and contributed to the effective, subdued sense of style Calla created without a second's thought.

"Good morning, Calla," he said softly, his gaze lingering on her lips. She could see the memory of last night in his gaze and smiled back, her confidence bounding effortlessly upward.

He walked toward her and she thought he was going to kiss her but he didn't. Instead he indicated a chair and she slipped into it. There was a watchful look in his expression and she wondered humorously what he was thinking. He must be wondering why she was here this morning.

He leaned back against the desk, folding his arms across his chest and waited.

"I'm on my way to work," she said quietly, her eyes smiling. "I only stopped by for a minute to see you."

"Calla, my sweet," he grinned suddenly, "you never do

164

anything without a reason. Correct me if I'm wrong, but I get the feeling this isn't merely a social call, right?"

Her smile widened. "Well, in certain respects it is. I've come to tell you I'm accepting your proposal of marriage, Slade."

She waited with breathless confidence and anticipation for him to whirl her around the room in his arms or something equally enthusiastic.

But all she got was a faint inclination of his dark head. "I see."

Calla blinked and felt the first tendrils of fear. Surely she hadn't mistaken his feelings for her? No. There could be no doubt. Not after last night . . .

A little nervously she got to her feet and walked away from him toward the window.

"I . . . I think we could have a good marriage, Slade. I'm willing to try and I think we can work out the one or two little problems that remain . . ."

"Do you?"

Calla realized with a start she was coming to hate it when he said those two words in that tone of voice. But she was committed now.

"Yes, I do. I realize you still feel a little possessive . . ."

"A little?"

She wasn't looking at him but she could see the arched eyebrow in her mind's eye.

"But I've decided that's normal after your experience with your first wife. In time you'll see that jealousy and possessiveness have no place in a good marriage. Our relationship will be based on trust and understanding, Slade."

"You don't think you might suffer from a little possessiveness yourself?" he asked with seemingly mild interest.

She smiled benignly out the window, her eyes on the

165

horizon. "I trust you, Slade. I haven't trusted any man for a long time, but I trust you."

"I've told you before, that doesn't have much to do with possessiveness."

"But it does. And someday soon, I think you'll realize that," she said impulsively, swinging around to look at him with loving eyes.

He was watching her with a hooded gaze that she couldn't fathom.

"You're basing that assumption on what happened last night, aren't you?" he asked shrewdly. "You think because you were in control last night that you can control other aspects of the marriage, don't you?"

"Slade . . ." Apprehension entered her mind for the first time that morning. She had been so certain . . .

"Tell me again exactly what you want out of this marriage," he rasped softly, not moving.

"But you already know!"

"I want to know exactly what I'm getting into," he grated. "So tell me again."

"I want trust and understanding and mutual respect . . ." she began falteringly, no longer sure at all of his mood. What was going wrong this morning?

"But you want no part of the passionate side of things, is that it?" he pressed heavily, his eyes narrowing. "You can't accept my possessiveness or jealousy, nor experience them in return, right? You can't accept that between a man and a woman things aren't always logical, rational, or civilized. That sometimes a man might feel like putting his woman in chains regardless of how much he trusts her. That a woman might be capable of the same kind of possessiveness. You want a milk-and-water relationship without any of the uncivilized strings attached, don't you?"

166

"Slade, you don't understand . . ." she began helplessly, apprehension turning to outright fear.

"I understand. You want a businesslike marriage with, now that you've discovered the full extent of it, a little sex thrown in on the side," he said harshly, his metallic gaze raking her taut features. "Well, I'm glad that physically you got what you wanted last night, Calla, but that's not a good enough reason for us to get married! I find your latest negotiating terms unacceptable! The kind of marriage you're offering isn't what I want."

And then she understood. Stunned at the enormity of her mistake, Calla felt the blood drain from her face as she stared in shock at the hard man across from her.

She had failed him last night. She hadn't satisfied him after all. The pleasure she had sought to give as well as to take had fallen short of its goal. Just as she should have known it would.

Hadn't she learned anything at all four years ago?

CHAPTER TEN

"I think," Calla finally managed with a gallows humor that amazed her, "I'm learning what it feels like to wish the floor under my feet would simply disappear and allow me to make a dignified exit!"

She turned away a little blindly, searching for the door. It took every drop of four years of discipline to traverse the short distance without crumpling into a heap but she had almost made it when Slade bit out her name.

"Calla! Wait . . ."

She paused at the door, bracing herself with a death grip on the knob, and summoned every scrap of pride. He was starting toward her now, his expression angry and determined.

"No!" It was a cry of distress that she masked immediately with a dazzling smile that never reached her eyes. "I mean there's absolutely no need to explain any further. I should have understood at once. With my track record I should have understood last night! But I seem to be a slow learner about some matters."

He halted, searching her face as if trying to comprehend what she was saying.

"Calla, listen to me . . ."

"It's all right, Slade. Believe me, you were a lot more polite about it than my ex-husband was! I'm very grateful for the way you waited until this morning. I'm a morning person, you know," she went on with a horrifying chattiness. "I'm much stronger then. Able to leap tall buildings in a single bound some days."

"What the hell are you talking about?" he growled.

"Don't pay any attention, I'm rambling," she assured

him brightly. "Well, I've got to be on my way. My secretary will be wondering where I am and I . . ."

"Calla, stop!"

But she was already out the door, whizzing briskly past a startled Mrs. Cosgrove and heading for the exit with a single-minded determination that would have made the author of the self-help book she'd been reading quite proud.

"Mr. York, don't forget your nine o'clock meeting. . . ."

"Tell them I might be a little late."

Calla didn't hear anything more. She was hurrying along the hall and out the swinging doors toward where the Fiat waited.

"Calla!"

She dug her keys out of her purse and broke into a run when she was only a few feet from the car. But he caught up with her, snagging her wrist and yanking her to a halt in front of him.

"Dammit! I do not like being seen chasing my female executives through the parking lot!" he roared furiously.

"No one asked you to come after me! You've already said what you have to say!"

"Somehow I get the feeling there's a serious communication gap here!"

"Not at all! I'm a little slow, as I've admitted, but once I have a point driven home in no uncertain terms, I eventually catch on like everyone else!"

Calla faced him, her head high, her eyes glittering with unshed tears. Not for anything would she let those tears fall in front of him. She had her pride, dammit!

He gave her a small shake, and her hand holding the keys instinctively came up in defense. "Let me go!" she hissed, grasping the keys the way she had been taught last year in a woman's self-defense class.

170

"Not until you explain exactly what you were talking about in my office!" he rasped, paying no attention to the threat of the keys. He was holding both her shoulders in a bruising grip and his face was a mask of anger and male impatience.

"Now you're the one who's being a little slow on the uptake!" she flung back. "Or are you just being cruel? That's it, isn't it?" she whispered hoarsely. "You're determined to make me admit the full depths of my failure! I wouldn't have thought it of you, Slade! I didn't think you were the type to kick someone after she was already down!"

"Calla, just shut up and explain yourself!"

"I can't do both. Either I shut up or I explain. The two are mutually exclusive!"

"Get in the car. I don't want the crowd at the windows watching us."

He took the keys out of her hand and wrenched open the door of the small car, thrusting her into the seat and sliding in beside her.

"Now what in hell was that all about in my office!"

She glanced pointedly at her digital watch. "You've got a management meeting, remember?"

"I've got a major management crisis going on right here! It comes first. Now talk, Calla Nevin. This is your last warning."

She shrugged, shifting her gaze out the window, away from his cold, hard face. "What more do you want from me, Slade? I'm sorry I embarrassed you by coming to your office this morning, but if it's any consolation, I can promise you I'm literally mortified."

"Because I said I wouldn't marry you on your terms?" he prodded ruthlessly.

"You can't blame me for not knowing there would still be strings attached to the proposal. I thought . . ." She

171

swallowed carefully, still not looking at him. "I was silly enough to think that you'd still want to marry me after last night. I didn't realize I hadn't . . . That is, you didn't . . ."

She bit furiously down on her lower lip to stop the stupid flow of words. She certainly didn't owe this man any sort of explanation! He already knew she'd failed.

"Calla, let's take this from the top one more time, okay?" he gritted with a mockery of patience. "I was under the impression that last night you learned something about physical satisfaction. Something you hadn't known before, right? Don't tell me you faked it because I won't believe it. No woman could fake it that well!"

She frowned, darting him an uncertain glance. "Fake what? I didn't fake anything! Is that another accusation you're going to hurl at me this morning?"

Slade sucked in his breath with barely restrained temper. His eyes glittered with the emotion as he sat facing her with one arm flung along the back of the bucket seat.

"So you did find satisfaction last night!"

Calla's temper began to feed her struggling pride. "If you're looking for a testimonial regarding your ability as a lover, I'll be glad to put it in writing on office letterhead!"

"I only want to establish that you found what you were looking for last night. . . ."

"But I didn't," she whispered sadly, her fingers tightening together in her lap.

"Dammit, Calla! You just finished saying . . ."

"Slade, I didn't go to bed with you last night with the objective of finding out what female satisfaction is like. I wasn't even thinking about it," Calla said wearily.

"Then what, exactly, was the nature of the experiment you were conducting?" he ground out between clenched teeth.

"There was no experiment. At least, I didn't think of it

172

in those terms until you made a joke of it. You see, I was foolish enough to have reached the point where I was sure I could make you happy. I was feeling quite certain of myself when I asked you to stay last night. I wasn't experimenting," she ended lamely.

"Oh, my God!" he muttered thickly. His hand snapped out and captured her firm little chin, forcing her around to meet his eyes. "What did that man do to you, anyway?"

"Drew?" she mumbled, not pretending to misunderstand. "He made it very clear I wasn't . . . that I wasn't capable of satisfying a man completely. I thought from the way you had been reacting during the past few days that maybe with you things would be different. I wanted to make you happy, Slade. It's that simple. And that impossible, apparently."

He swore emphatically and violently. "Calla, for God's sake, believe me! I had no idea you had any doubts on that score whatsoever! How could I? I told you once that you're like a fire under the sea and last night I got close enough to be totally consumed by the flames! Satisfied! Listen to me, sweetheart, this morning when I left, I could hardly walk out to the car! You're a wild little thing when you come alive in a man's arms. You make him want to tame you and then let you go wild again for the sheer satisfaction of repeating the taming! Of course I was satisfied, you little idiot! And I had the added pleasure of knowing I'd satisfied you, too! How was I to know I'd misdiagnosed your particular hangup? Why didn't you explain it to me?"

Calla held herself aloofly away from him, afraid to give in to the vast relief she was feeling until she knew for certain where the conversation was going.

"It isn't the sort of thing one likes to discuss with a man," she offered distantly.

"But you knew I assumed we were involved with showing you the range of your own emotions," he accused almost gently.

"Well, what was wrong with that assumption?" she tried to say with dignity. "It was the truth as far as it went. I hadn't ever . . . I mean . . ."

"Skip it. Don't you know the old saying? There are no frigid women, only inept men!" His teeth showed very whitely in a tight grin that came and went quickly. "I figured your problem was that you needed to feel in control of the situation. I thought maybe you'd felt used by that ex-husband of yours and it had ruined your chances at physical pleasure. Then, I had to come on like a ton of bricks that first time I kissed you . . . ! I cursed myself for a fool that night after I left you, did you know that? I called myself every name in the book for having rushed you and, in the process, probably scaring you."

"I wasn't frightened!" she snapped, goaded.

He dismissed that. "I told myself you needed to feel in charge until your confidence in yourself was restored. But I was thinking of confidence in your ability to receive a full measure of satisfaction. I didn't realize you were functioning under the double whammy of doubting your ability to satisfy your partner, too!"

"Well, now you know," she said bleakly. "I don't see its impact on the situation very much. You still said my . . . my terms for marriage weren't acceptable!"

The rugged face softened and the golden eyes warmed. "Honey, I didn't say that I wasn't going to marry you. But I want you too much to take you on the washed-out, businesslike terms you offered when you walked into my office a few minutes ago! I told you I've got my pride, too!"

Calla was discovering that temper was a nice alternative to the devastating humiliation she'd just been through. She didn't want to stop now and give Slade credit for at least rescuing her from that, however.

"If you're going to insist on talking about this in business language let me assure you that treating me as you did this morning isn't going to improve your bargaining position one bit! Do you have any idea what it does to a woman to go to bed with a man who's said he wants to marry her and then have him renege on the proposal the next morning? The fact that I'm thirty years old doesn't give me some sort of immunity to humiliation!"

"But I didn't understand everything going on in that raging little brain of yours, dammit! Don't you see? I was only trying to jolt you into a realization of my needs . . ."

"Consider me jolted!" Calla once again slanted a grim glance at her watch. "You'd better be getting to that meeting, Slade."

"You're not my secretary. You don't have to feel obliged to keep reminding me!" he snarled.

"I believe we were speaking of pride a moment ago. Both yours and mine are going to be affected when your staff finds out you're sitting out in the parking lot instead of conducting a management meeting!"

"Don't you dare give me that queen-chastising-the-local-peasant routine," he warned. But she could see the gathering frustration in him and told herself it served him right.

"Why not?" she jibed. "Your threats are singularly limited at the moment. You already know I'm not particular about keeping my job and you've told me you're not going to marry me. I don't see that you have anything left to use against me," she drawled sweetly.

His hand went to the door handle with a sharp, aggressive movement.

"We will discuss this tonight," he told her with the full force of the presidential position of York Instruments. "I will meet you at your place after work!"

He climbed out of the car and slammed the door shut, leaning down to continue the warning through the open window.

"We're going to hammer this thing out between us if it takes all night!"

"Some things aren't negotiable, Slade!"

"Nonsense," he countered gruffly, straightening. "You and I have had a great deal of practice in negotiating. We'll work something out." He turned and stalked off through the parking lot.

Seething, Calla threw the Fiat into reverse and raced out of the parking lot. There could be no doubt about going down to that weekend seminar in Tucson. It had been a long time since she'd needed to get away from a situation and think but that was precisely what the current state of affairs demanded.

If she left early this afternoon she would be at the convention resort in time for the welcoming cocktail hour. It would be a way of taking her mind off the uncertain fate that awaited her if she chose to stay docilely at home, she decided with a vengeance.

Several hours later Calla was driving down the freeway. So he didn't like her terms? Well, he should have thought of that before he'd decided he wanted to marry her! She had never deceived him about the sort of relationship she wanted with a man! No, he had been the one to deceive her!

He'd been quite willing to go to bed with her without any "terms," she reminded herself with angry impatience. It was only when it came to making good on his proposal of marriage that Slade York grew suddenly very business-like about the whole matter. Typical York approach. She should have known better than to get involved with the man. A month sitting across the negotiating table from him should have taught her something about how his mind worked!

The two-hour trip to the Tucson resort went by in a haze of self-recrimination and grim self-defense. By the time Calla had checked into the luxurious room and picked up the packet of information available for workshop attendees, she was ready for a shower and an interlude of forgetfulness. The latter, she hoped, would be provided by the necessary socializing at the cocktail hour organized for the participants.

She dressed for it with care, feeling the need to rebuild a facade that had weakened badly during the past few days. She chose the black halter-neck gown she had worn the night at the country club, knowing the stark simplicity added to the sophisticated, totally in-control look she wanted to achieve. Brushing her hair back into a sleek coil at the nape, she added tiny crystal earrings and pronounced herself satisfied. Stepping into heeled black sandals, she grabbed a small, black-beaded clutch purse and headed downstairs.

Her cool, poised entrance into the milling throng of fellow attendees drew several interested glances, which she ignored with casual ease. It also produced several welcoming smiles from friends and associates. These Calla returned. A drink was politely thrust into her hand and she was soon absorbed into the cheerful group.

"Calla! Glad you could make it," Sandra Miller sang out happily, waving to her friend. Sandra worked at another firm in Phoenix and the two women had met at several local technical meetings. "Come over here and help me hold my own with this crowd. There are still too many men in our line of work. The proportions are all wrong!"

Calla smiled a little distantly at the circle of grinning male faces surrounding the attractive redheaded engineer.

177

"You can say that again, Sandy. Introduce us to your friend!" one of the males demanded with a friendly leer that Calla instantly resented.

"This is Calla Nevin. She was a manager at Chapman, Inc. in Phoenix," Sandra began helpfully.

"Was?" the man who had demanded the introduction asked carefully, some of his obvious interest fading from his gray eyes at the words "manager." Calla could almost see his wariness. Another man who exercised extreme caution around successful women, she thought with a mild disgust. But she kept her face composed and pleasant.

"Chapman, Inc. has been acquired by York Instruments," she explained coolly. "Management titles are in a state of flux. York really doesn't need another manager of planning and resources."

"I see. Are you going to stay with the firm?"

"I doubt it."

"My name's Vance Ramsey, by the way. I'm with a test instrument firm here in Tucson." Vance was relaxing a bit now.

Calla acknowledged the introduction as the others in the group fell into a discussion on the microprocessor revolution in instrumentation. Vance was a good-looking man, somewhere in his thirties, with dark brown hair that lacked the rich color of Slade's and a body that was going a bit soft around the middle. He was dressed in a trendy sports coat and slacks and he clearly was aware of his own attractiveness.

"So you won't be staying with York? Any plans for the future?" her new acquaintance went on conversationally, swirling his drink with a negligent movement and giving Calla the full benefit of his rather nice gray eyes by stepping closer and drawing her slightly away from the rest of the group.

178

Calla gave a mental shrug and allowed him to affect the more intimate arrangement. She had come to this party to get away from thoughts of Slade, hadn't she? It was merely unfortunate that she couldn't look at Vance Ramsey without making comparisons. Comparisons that ruined whatever slight chance Vance might have had of holding her interest for much longer.

"I haven't decided yet what I'm going to do," she told Vance calmly and sipped at her drink. "I've had overtures in the past from a couple of other companies. I might reestablish contact with one of them and see if they're still interested."

He nodded. "Is York making any attempt to keep you?"

"York," announced a too-familiar, gritty masculine voice behind Calla, "is going out of its way to keep her!"

"Slade!" In spite of herself, Calla whirled around in astonishment to confront his glittering amber eyes. "What are you doing here?"

"Close your mouth, honey, it isn't good for a lady executive to look as if she's been caught in a compromising position!" he advised in a soft drawl.

"You're a friend of Calla's?" Vance asked warily, eyeing the older man with slightly narrowed eyes.

"You could say that. I'm Slade York. Her boss."

"I see. Well, I expect you two have business to discuss," Vance said glibly, not failing to take in the full effect of Slade's barely leashed aggression. He knew when he was outranked and out of his league. "I'll see you later, Calla. Nice to meet you. . . ."

Calla hardly noticed as her new acquaintance slipped back into the crowd. Her full attention was on Slade, as he stood facing her with challenge in every square inch of the lean, hard frame. He was still wearing the gray business suit he'd had on earlier that morning.

179

"Well?" she demanded haughtily, deciding offense was always preferable to defense. Her head lifted automatically and the sea-colored eyes were layered with blue-green frost.

"Well, what? Enjoying yourself with your latest flirtation?" he countered. He was holding a glass of Scotch in one hand and propping himself against the wall with the other. Somehow Calla seemed to have become trapped against that wall.

"I wasn't flirting!" she denied irritably. "My God, Slade! You really do carry possessiveness to the heights of absurdity, don't you?"

"I can recognize when another man is on the make, if that's what you mean," he said coldly. "I didn't notice you trying to freeze him, either. What's the matter? Did last night whet your appetite, Calla? Did it make you wonder what you've been missing?"

Calla went quite white under the blow. "Always the gentleman, aren't you, Slade?" she whispered, her eyes holding his very bravely.

"Oh, hell!" he muttered in disgust. "I shouldn't have said that. I'm sorry, sweetheart, but when I found out you'd left the office early today and I realized you weren't going to meet me after work I was ready to come down here and drag you home in chains. It didn't do my mood much good to walk in and find you already paired off with some other male, either!"

Calla experienced a curious surge of excitement at his words. Instantly she dampened it. What was the matter with her? The last thing she needed was a jealous, immature male who claimed he wanted her. But she'd never had a man chase after her like this. There was an undeniable flicker of primitive female satisfaction at the knowledge.

"What are you going to do now that you've found me?

Still contemplating dragging me off in chains?" she taunted, aware of being unable to completely stifle that strange
pleasure she had known when she'd heard his voice.

"I'm going to make every effort to deal with you on a
rational, logical, *civilized* basis," he growled. "I made myself say it a hundred times on the way down here. I'm here
to attend the conference with you and I intend to use the
time to try and work on those negotiations we were supposed to be conducting!"

"You sound as if it's going to be a severe test of your
willpower!"

"It will be!"

"Should I be honored at the effort you're making?" she
provoked, wondering now what was driving her. Was she
going crazy?

"If you have any sense, Calla, you won't deliberately try
and make me forget all my good intentions," he warned
softly, and took a long swallow of the Scotch.

"How far can I trust those good intentions?"

"I'm trying to be reasonable, dammit! Can't you get
that through your head? I'm sorry about what happened
this morning. I admit I didn't handle the situation properly but that was because I was thinking of my own needs,
too! I thought we'd solved your basic problems last night
and could work on mine for a while!"

"Solved my basic problems!" she yelped in astounded
fury. "How typical of a man to think he can handle a
woman with sex! Of all the overbearing, conceited, arrogant . . ."

"Slade, darling! You made it down for the conference
after all! I'm so glad!"

Calla's tirade was trampled beneath the delighted cry.
She watched in amazement as a stunning blonde in her
late twenties swept down on Slade and threw her arms

around his neck. The woman was beautiful. The silver-blond hair was free and sexy in a wind-blown style; the slinky, off-the-shoulder red gown fully displayed a wealth of cleavage. The hazel eyes were exotically made-up and there was a bold, sultry pout to the shining red mouth.

The shining red mouth was planted firmly on Slade's at the moment and Calla was unaware of the way her nails were curving into her palm until the pain called her attention to the fact.

Slade, after a second's startled stiffness, relaxed, holding his Scotch carefully aside as he returned the kiss.

"Hello, Brenda," he said politely when his lips were freed. "I'm glad to see you. Let me introduce you to a . . . colleague of mine, Calla Nevin."

"How do you do, Calla?" Brenda said chattily as she removed one arm from around Slade's neck and left the other clinging to his shoulder. The hazel eyes made a quick assessment of the other woman and then relaxed. The rest of Brenda relaxed, too, Calla noted, right against Slade's side.

"Do you work with Slade?" the blonde continued interestedly.

"I work for him," Calla corrected smoothly, her hand tightening on her glass. A colleague, hmm?

"Oh, I see." Brenda seemed to lose interest almost at once as she turned back to Slade. "I must admit I'm surprised to see you. I thought you always hated this sort of gathering! What brought you down this time? Not that I'm complaining."

"I, uh, thought I'd better catch the seminar on MATS," he explained easily, his amber eyes on the blonde's face.

Mobile Automatic Test Systems? Calla grimaced at the lie. He certainly hadn't shown any interest in the subject before Brenda's arrival. Slade had come to this conference to find Calla, not a lecture on the current developments in on-site testing of airplane instruments!

"Fantastic!" Brenda approved smilingly. "That's my main interest here, too. Have you had a chance to view the displays?"

"Not yet. Just arrived a few minutes ago."

"Oh, then you haven't had dinner yet, I'll bet!"

"No, as a matter of fact . . ." Slade began mildly.

"Slade and I were just about to go into the restaurant, Brenda. I'm sure you'll excuse us?" Calla heard herself say.

In the second of startled silence Calla only had time to ask herself bitterly for an explanation of her own words before she met Slade's deceptively bland gaze. Well, damn him, he'd come down here to talk about their relationship, hadn't he? How did he expect to do it if he spent his time amusing Brenda? Her eyes challenged him aloofly, daring him to deny her statement to the other woman.

"Oh, Slade . . . ?" The red lips pouted prettily.

"Uh, I'm afraid Calla's right. We were on our way in to dinner. Perhaps you'll join us for a drink afterward?" he added hopefully. "We'll probably be in the lounge."

"Count on it!" Brenda smiled brilliantly, going up on her toes again to brush his mouth tantalizingly with her own. "I'll see you both later."

Calla watched the tight-fitting red dress disappear into a crowd of dark suits across the room.

"Brenda who?" she asked a little tightly.

"Oh, I forgot to mention a last name, didn't I?" Slade murmured politely, his eyes on her frowning profile. "That's Brenda Meredith. Known her for years. She used to work in Phoenix before moving to Tucson."

"Where did she work in Phoenix?"

"York Instruments," he said quite neutrally.

"I see."

"Do you?"

"I wish you wouldn't say that," Calla informed him in annoyance.

"Sorry. How about: You do?"

"For a man who claims he's trying to be reasonable tonight, you're not making great progress in the right direction. Are you coming in to dinner or not?"

"I'm starving." He took her arm and led her through the crowd toward the resort restaurant on the other side of the modernistically western-styled lobby.

"You don't have to worry about Brenda, you know," he said carefully as he seated her a few minutes later in the red and gold dining room.

"I wasn't worried about her in the least. Why should I? She looks like a woman who can take care of herself!" Calla picked up the menu and propped it in front of her face.

She heard Slade opening the leather case he'd taken from his pocket.

"It had occurred to me you might be wondering about my, uh, association with her," he explained calmly.

"Not at all. I thought she made her association with you quite clear!" Calla was proud of the distant hauteur in her voice. It didn't reflect the angry trembling in her fingertips at all.

"She's only a friend, Calla." There was a suspended element in the slightly roughened voice. "You know how it is with old friends . . ."

Calla's menu went down on the white tablecloth with a snap and she met Slade's blandly inquiring gaze with an intense, no-nonsense glare that she used only in the most extreme situations at work.

"I could care less about your old 'friends,' Slade York! But I want to make it very clear that if you've really

184

followed me down here in an effort to engage in a reasonable and civilized discussion of our relationship, you can
forget about inviting Brenda Meredith to join us! The sort
of discussion we're supposed to be having doesn't require
third parties. Get rid of her!"

CHAPTER ELEVEN

The amber gaze flamed slightly behind the dark-rimmed glasses but Slade's expression was one of calm, his voice that of the totally reasonable male. Deliberately he lowered his menu and studied her regally set features.

"Doesn't it occur to you that you're the one who's beginning to sound a trifle less than reasonable and civilized? I've already explained about Brenda. And you've said on more than one occasion that you trust me. . . ."

"It's got nothing to do with trust . . . !"

Calla broke off, stricken to the core by her own words. They were a clear imitation of what he, himself, had said often enough. Desperately she sought to regain her self-discipline.

"I mean," she pursued valiantly, "that as you claim you only drove down here to talk to me, it doesn't make much sense to socialize."

"You wouldn't have me be rude, would you?"

"I'm sure that with all your experience as president of a large company you have the resources for practical diplomacy at your fingertips," she muttered, lifting her menu once again and frowning down at it severely.

"I shall try to handle it as well as you've handled Crispin and that man you were talking with when I found you a little while ago," he told her suavely.

"Don't tease me, Slade. This is serious!"

"I couldn't agree more. Shall I choose the wine?"

"As long as you choose a '74 Napa Valley Cabernet or a '77 North Coast Zinfandel!"

"Your faith in my taste leaves me breathless," Slade said dryly. "I'll try to surprise you with one or the other."

It took an effort but Calla managed to get her temper back under control during dinner. It was chiefly the thought of how unexpectedly it had flared out of bounds that subdued her. She knew she had reacted to Brenda Meredith with unreasoning dislike and there was absolutely no excuse for it. The blonde was only a friend of Slade's, wasn't she?

Dinner passed in a state of armed neutrality. Calla went out of her way to maintain a polite, eminently reasonable facade and was annoyed when it became obvious that Slade's civilized behavior was entirely natural. Was he no longer upset about finding her talking to Vance Ramsey?

"I noticed there's a workshop on the Quality Circle technique being held in the morning," he observed conversationally at one point. "Perhaps I should take it in as long as I'm here. It will give me a better framework from which to judge the QCs you've established."

"An excellent idea," Calla approved a bit stiltedly. "I'm going to be attending that discussion myself."

It was touch and go but by the time they left the table and headed for the lounge, Calla felt she had herself back under control. When was Slade going to begin to talk about the real reason he'd pursued her to Tucson? So far all they had discussed was work.

They had no sooner claimed a small table in the lounge and ordered after-dinner liqueurs than Brenda Meredith glided toward them from out of the gloom.

"I thought you two would never get here!" she exclaimed merrily. She had Vance Ramsey in tow. "Vance, darling, dance with Calla, will you? It's been ages since I've had a chance to dance with Slade!"

Calla watched Slade politely allow himself to be led away and recognized her instinct for what it was. She wanted to put up "Keep Off" signs. She wanted to brand him for her own so that other women wouldn't casually claim him for a dance or a kiss or anything else. She wanted . . .

"You will join me on the floor, won't you, Calla?" Vance interrupted her thoughts to inquire charmingly. He was extending a hand to assist her gallantly to her feet.

"Of course," she said with great dignity.

But on the floor it was all she could do to keep from glaring pointedly at the other couple. Brenda was laughing beautifully up into Slade's attentive face and the blonde's arms were once more wrapped around his neck.

"I got the impression York might be more than your employer," Vance was saying delicately as he took Calla into his arms. "But he seems quite happy to be dancing with Brenda. Can I take that to mean you're not earmarked for the boss?"

Calla's head snapped around angrily. "What a terrible expression! I'm certainly not Slade's private property! He's my boss for the time being but even that's not going to last long!"

"Okay, okay!" Vance chuckled. "Just making sure before I put my foot in it!"

Calla forced a smile. "Brenda is an old friend of his," she tried experimentally.

"Brenda is an old friend of a lot of folks," Vance grinned. "I'm hoping she'll be my old friend one of these days, too. Unless you're interested in the job?"

On the edge of quelling him with an icy gaze, Calla called off the put-down at the last instant. She caught sight of Brenda's blond head nestled against Slade's gray jacket and found herself smiling up at Vance, instead of chilling him with a few choice remarks.

"Funny you should mention a job . . ." she murmured lightly.

"That's right. You're going to be needing one soon, aren't you?" he chuckled, pulling her closer. Calla let him do it, not enjoying the feel of being so close to his body but taking a strange comfort in the look she'd spotted in Slade's eyes when he saw what was happening.

When she saw that Brenda had managed to keep Slade out on the floor for a second dance, Calla allowed Vance the same privilege and it was some time before both couples were reunited at the table.

Calla sat down quickly, as much to remove the feel of Vance's fingers from her bare back as anything else. She hid a shiver of distaste and tried to hope that the encounter on the floor had been worth it.

Worth it! What was the matter with her? Was this outright jealousy? She loved Slade York and, in spite of his behavior, deep down she trusted him, too! So what was happening here tonight?

Somehow she found herself sitting much closer to Vance than to Slade and Calla realized grimly that Brenda had subtly shifted the pattern. Why wasn't Slade doing something about it? This was supposed to be her evening with him, not the blonde's.

"Did you know Calla was going to be looking for a job, soon?" Vance was saying smoothly to Brenda. He didn't look as if he particularly cared which woman he wound up with so long as he had a date for the evening.

"You're going to be leaving York Instruments?" Brenda asked coolly, not displaying a great deal of interest one way or the other.

"In all probability," Calla affirmed frostily. "I'm only staying on long enough to assist during the transition process."

"I had a job on my hands convincing Calla to remain," Slade interposed easily, seemingly content to have Brenda's fingertips on his sleeve in that proprietary fashion.

"I'm trying to convince her there are other possibilities in the world, myself," Vance grinned.

"I'll give you a clue on handling her," Slade offered neutrally. "She's amenable to a little old-fashioned blackmail when all attempts at reasoning fail."

"Slade!" Calla's outraged gasp barely drew his attention. He was too busy ordering a drink for Brenda.

"I'll remember that," Vance laughed.

"Just don't put yourself into a bargaining position with her," Slade went on to advise as the cocktail waitress left the table. "She likes terms that are only favorable to herself."

"What have the two of you bargained about?" Brenda demanded while Calla shot a seething glance at Slade's blank face.

"She handled the negotiations for Chapman, Inc., a firm York Instruments recently acquired."

"You handled the talks?" Vance demanded in astonishment, a trace of unease appearing in his handsome gray eyes.

"An aggressive, hard-headed businesswoman, you can take my word for it," Slade told him silkily.

"Mr. York is teasing you, Vance," Calla finally managed to say defensively, lifting her glass for a long sip. Her eyes were iceberg-cluttered seas as she met Slade's gaze over the rim.

"Mr. York never resorts to teasing the opposition," Slade countered. "He leaves that tactic for others."

"Mr. York prefers more direct methods such as the martial arts!" Calla snapped back without thinking.

"Subtlety is lost on some women."

"A statement made by men who don't know how to deal with the female of the species on a basis of equality."

"Such an accusation is the last intellectual line of defense left to a woman who is losing an argument," Slade explained to their two appalled listeners.

"It at least has the merit of being an *intellectual* line of defense instead of one that relies on brute force and uncivilized emotion!" Calla proclaimed arrogantly, her rage barely held in restraint. Never had she been so angry!

"Miss Nevin doesn't have a high opinion of some of the more primitive instincts and emotions involved in human relationships!" Slade grated.

"Mr. York seems to think such primitive emotions and instincts should be accepted and indulged simply because they exist. He has no respect for the use of civilized, rational behavior as a means of controlling those instincts and emotions so that a higher, more meaningful relationship can exist!"

"Miss Nevin's definition of a higher, more meaningful relationship is one in which she's in complete control!"

Oblivious to Brenda's and Vance's astonished stares, Calla countered, "Like most men, Mr. York can't abide the idea of a woman in command of anything!"

"Miss Nevin recently experienced a taste of feminine power and it went to her head," Slade murmured kindly. "She thinks she can have her cake and eat it, too."

"Mr. York is terrified he's created a monster."

"There's not much doubt of it!" Slade admitted briefly, eyes flaming.

"As usual, he prefers to take credit for everything!"

"I also accept my responsibilities. Having created the monster, I shall have to tame it!"

In desperation Brenda broke in, her hand clutching at Slade's. "Listen, they're playing another dance. Let's go, Slade!"

Calla watched her victim being led away through slitted eyes, her lashes barely concealing the roiling seas of her gaze from Vance, who nervously did his duty.

"Would you, uh, like to dance again, Calla?"

She flicked him a disinterested look and realized the poor man was quite frightened of her.

"I'd love to," she told him maliciously, rising lightly to her feet.

"Boy!" he mumbled on the floor, holding her this time as if she were a living bomb. "You two don't get along very well, do you? No wonder you're looking for another job!"

Calla responded uncommunicatively, her eyes on the couple across the floor.

Three dances and another drink later Slade glared at Calla, who was sitting closer than ever to Vance, this time of her own accord. She could find no other way to retaliate than in kind, and after the argument earlier, Brenda had not made the mistake of leaving Slade open to another such attack. The blonde was entirely too protective as far as Calla was concerned. Slade could take care of himself.

"Do you think you can tear yourself away from your 'friend' long enough to honor your boss with a dance, Calla?" It was a direct challenge, not an invitation.

"The question is whether or not your 'friend' can get her hand off you long enough to let you try going out on the dance floor without her assistance," Calla retorted gently.

"I'm sure you two will excuse us," Slade grated to Vance and Brenda as he got to his feet and reached for Calla's wrist.

She was virtually hauled into his arms with an impact that made her gasp.

"Not exactly light on your feet, are you?" he rapped as she stumbled against him. "I mean, considering you're a dancer and all . . ."

"I think I'll manage if you'll keep the judo exhibition until a more appropriate time!"

"Does poor Ramsey know you're not going back to his

room with him tonight or are you leading the guy on until it's too late and you find yourself with a major scene on your hands?" he inquired pleasantly, ignoring the comment on judo.

"The only one creating a scene tonight is you!" she stormed through her teeth. She felt his hand tense on her bare lower back. "And I was under the impression you came down here to be reasonable!"

"I tried. So help me, God, I tried! You've been behaving like a first-class little hell cat since Brenda appeared!"

"You'll forgive me, I'm sure, when I explain that I've had a rough day. I think it began this morning when I found out the man who had proposed to me had changed his mind!"

"And, added to that, naturally, was the fact that you didn't get much sleep last night," he offered kindly.

Calla ignored that sally. What else could she do? Just one more infuriating remark for which he would someday pay. Instead she went on thoughtfully, "Things deteriorated steadily until this evening, when you showed up claiming you'd followed me down here to discuss our relationship in a reasonable manner. But you haven't had a chance to do that because you've been too busy flirting with that blond 'friend' of yours!"

"You're getting a little loud," Slade noted. "Would you care to step outside to finish this discussion?"

"What's left to discuss?" Calla asked airily.

"Your behavior, perhaps?" he suggested helpfully. "Now that you've dissected mine it seems the least we can do!"

Without giving her a chance to argue further, Slade used a hand forcefully against her lower spine and steered her out of the lounge and onto the terraced patio, which surrounded an elegant pool.

"We seem fated to keep returning to this sort of set-

194

ting," he observed with a resigned sigh as he glanced around the silent, attractively lit pool.

"If you're going to bring up last night again . . . !"

"No, I wasn't. I was referring to that night at the country club after the acquisition papers had been signed, remember?"

"How could I forget?" Calla muttered tartly. "Now, about Brenda . . ."

"What about her? I've told you she's merely an old friend . . ."

"Who's acting like an old lover who wants to take up where she left off!"

"If that's the way you see it," he soothed, pacing lazily around the meandering pool.

"I do." Calla fell into step beside him, frowning.

"Well, I can't honestly blame you," Slade admitted judiciously, not looking at her. "I, myself, am apt to get upset about some of your old friends from time to time. Some of your newer friends, too," he concluded with an air of great truthfulness.

Calla shot him a suspicious glance. "My feelings about Brenda have nothing in common with your egotistical possessiveness!"

"Liar," he drawled laconically.

"Slade York, I am not going to listen to another minute of your ridiculous analysis of the situation! Either get rid of that woman and concentrate on the reason you're supposed to be here or I'll . . ."

"You'll what?" he inquired interestedly, turning his head to regard her with an expression of rapt attention. "As I see it there's not much you can do and still remain true to your esoteric belief in a fine and noble relationship between a man and a woman that is carried out on a higher plane of existence. One that isn't tainted by such base emotions as possessiveness or jealousy."

195

She stared at him, speechless with helpless fury. How dare he imply her feelings were motivated by the sort of immature possessiveness that he claimed was normal? Worse yet, how dare he be right?

"No, as I see it," Slade continued obligingly, his gaze focused absently in the middle distance ahead of him, "you're stuck with having to accord me all the rights and privileges you want me to accord you. Otherwise your whole philosophical framework breaks down, doesn't it? To put it more crudely, what's sauce for the goose, is sauce for the . . ."

"Slade York," Calla began in icy tones, "you're an arrogant, egotistical devil and you've had this coming for well over a month!"

Without giving any warning of her intentions Calla reached out with both hands, a dancer's sense of balance, and a focused willpower that would have amazed the author of her latest self-help book.

She pushed Slade into the pool.

He went in with a huge, frothy splash and a strangled yelp that was rudely cut off as he plunged beneath the surface of the crystal green water.

Calla stood on the edge and watched as a wave of pure female satisfaction washed over her. Some things in life were worth any amount of risk, she decided as Slade gathered himself under the water and shot back to the surface. He broke it with a savage flip of his head that sent his coffee dark hair flying back off his forehead.

The gray suit was undoubtedly ruined, Calla decided with a small pang. For some reason that was the first rational thought that forced its way into her consciousness after the initial adrenaline-produced exultation faded.

The second rational thought, engendered no doubt by a belated sense of self-preservation, was the realization that Slade was furious. His eyes met hers and she saw the blazing intent in the amber depths. He looked like a wet panther as he stroked cleanly for the side of the pool.

The urge to push him in had been irresistible. Calla didn't waste any time regretting it. But she absorbed the menace in the taut features, the crisp manner in which Slade was nearing the edge of the pool, and the masculine outrage that was radiating from him, and she picked up her black skirts and ran.

Unmindful of lost dignity or the danger of twisting an ankle in the heeled sandals, she raced across the lawn, heading for the outside entrance of her room.

A glance over one shoulder showed that Slade was out of the pool and had managed to divest himself of the sopping wet gray coat. He didn't seem to be hurrying but somehow his swift, stalking stride was eating up the distance between them with deliberate speed.

Her heels clattering on the stairs, Calla reached the second level of motel rooms and dug out her key as she neared her own. She could hear him on the steps behind her now and her fingers trembled as she shoved the key into the lock.

"You'll never make it, honey," he growled as he moved toward her. "And even if you did, it wouldn't do you much good. I've got another key."

Calla twisted the doorknob, knew he was right, and spun to face him boldly.

"Don't tell me you're the sort of man who stoops to getting even for every petty . . . Slade!"

He was on her in one last stride, shoving open the door and crowding her inside ahead of him. There was a very solid clunk as he kicked the door shut with one wet leather shoe.

Catching her balance, Calla backed steadily away from him, her wary eyes on his determined face. Instead of following her, his fingers went to the dripping tie and he yanked it off impatiently. Then he started to work on the buttons of his shirt.

"What do you think you're doing?" Calla hissed. "You can go back to your own room to change your clothes!"

"I've got more important matters at the moment," he gritted, peeling off the wet shirt and dropping it onto the floor. He went down on one knee and began undoing the laces of the black leather shoes.

"Such as?" she challenged bravely, determined not to let him terrorize her. But her heart was beginning to pound from something besides the exercise she had recently had.

He glanced up from his project. "Such as showing you what a reasonable male I am."

"What are you talking about, Slade? And you're getting the floor all wet!" she added inconsequentially.

"Whose fault is that?" He removed one shoe and transferred his attention to the other.

"Now listen to me, Slade York . . ."

"That's exactly what I plan to do. Listen to you. First I'm going to listen to you tell me why you pushed me into the pool . . ."

"I've already explained that! I did it before I pushed you!"

"I mean the real reason," he corrected imperturbably, slipping off the other shoe and rising to his feet to put them both on the tiled floor of the bath.

"I gave you the real reason! Your behavior was abominable this evening!"

"And after we've listened to that little discussion we're going to go to bed together like two rational, reasonable human beings who have managed to communicate."

"Not on your life!" she vowed.

He was still in the bathroom and she knew he was unbuckling his belt and stepping out of the gray slacks.

But he was watching her from the doorway and there would be no chance of making it out the front door before he reached her.

"Let's begin at the beginning, shall we?" he gritted, emerging from the bathroom with a towel wrapped carelessly around his waist and using another one to dry his shoulders and chest. He sank into the chair nearest the door and eyed her narrowly as she stood on the far side of the room.

"You have absolutely no right to be here. I demand that you leave at once!"

He dismissed that with a negligent wave of one large hand. "First things first. Why did you push me into the pool?"

"Because you are the most annoying, aggravating, provoking man I have ever had the misfortune to encounter!" she retorted, goaded.

He shook his head impatiently and leaned back in the chair, feet outstretched in front of him. There was a lazy, hooded look to the amber eyes that sent shivers down Calla's spine.

"Not good enough. Try again."

"That's as good an explanation as you're going to get!" she snarled.

"Nonsense. You can do much better. Shall I help you? I'll get you started. You arrived here this evening in a very nervous mood, didn't you? You were still upset over last night and my subsequent behavior this morning, right?"

"I certainly had every right to be upset!" she reminded him with a vengeance, wondering where this was leading.

He shrugged. "Perhaps. As I explained this morning, there was a misunderstanding involved. But we've already been through that. At any rate, you were in a high-strung frame of mind by this evening. You haven't had much sleep in the past twenty-four hours and you had a long drive down here late this afternoon."

"You sound as if you're building a case for temporary insanity!"

"Not quite. I'm explaining how it came to pass that all your defenses collapsed around you this evening. You were tired, tense, agitated, and feeling trapped . . ."

"Since you contributed heavily to my state of mind, I'm glad you appreciate the effect you had on me!"

"Oh, I do, I do," he agreed placatingly. "Very well, we have established that your mood was a precarious one at best. I'm willing to bet you were using the cocktail party as a mechanism to put some distance between yourself and your problems . . ."

"You're too understanding," Calla grated huskily, not moving from her very still pose across the room.

"I'm trying. Okay, into this situation we drop the first jolting encounter of the evening. Me. You have barely recovered from that intrusion when Brenda appears. That's when you started to lose control, isn't it, Calla? There, I've set it all up for you. All you have to do is finish the tale by explaining why you became irrational about my old acquaintance."

"I did not become irrational! You told me you'd come down here to talk to me and all you did was flirt with an old flame! Of course I was annoyed!"

"You were jealous as hell!" he shot back.

"No!"

"Yes, you were, dammit, and I'm going to make you admit it if it's the last thing I accomplish on this earth!"

Slade was suddenly on his feet in a lithe surge that took Calla by surprise. She tried to back farther away from him but there was no place to retreat. She stood straight and tense against the wall and watched his steady, relentless

200

approach as if she were the mesmerized victim of a hunting cat.

"Tell me, Calla!" he rasped, gliding to a halt only a foot away. "Tell me exactly what's been going through your crazy little head all evening!"

"Why didn't you get rid of her, Slade?" Calla wailed furiously, driven to her wits' end by the inquisition. "Why didn't you tell her to get lost?"

"Why should I have done that?" he flung back, golden eyes gleaming. "You haven't gone out of your way to steer clear of your old 'friends'!"

Knowing she really was coming apart at the seams and helpless to stop it, Calla swung her hand in a short, violent arc. Slade caught her wrist but otherwise ignored the desperate little attack.

"Why are you so upset tonight, Calla Nevin?" he pressed, his fingers like a handcuff around her wrist as he dragged it down to his side. "Don't you trust me?" he mocked.

Something seemed to explode inside her head. Calla flung up her chin proudly, all the fire he had once claimed to see in her blue-green eyes now blazing through the ice. Every line of her body was taut with a regal female pride and passion.

"That's got nothing to do with it! You're supposed to be mine, Slade York! You're not supposed to flirt with other women, damn you! You're supposed to let them know you're no longer available; that you belong to me! I can't bear to see other women looking you over like so much meat and then have you smile back at them while they do it! It didn't matter with Drew! Somehow, in the end, there was nothing left between us and it just didn't matter! I walked away from him without a second's regret. But I couldn't walk away from you like that!"

"And it scares you, doesn't it?" he concluded recklessly,

using the grip on her wrist to pull her closer. He raked her face with a searching, probing glance that took in everything from the passionate set of her mouth to the possessive, demanding blaze in her eyes. "It scares the hell out of you!"

"Yes! Yes, it does! Because I don't want it to become sick and destructive! I don't want . . ." She was close to tears now and only an effort of will kept them from falling.

"You don't want the possessiveness to do to us what it did to your first marriage," Slade finished abruptly, tugging her all the way into his arms and wrapping her close to his body. "But, sweetheart," he breathed in a gentling, soothing voice, "don't you see that this is not the same thing? We share a passion that demands everything of us, but it isn't destructive, it's protective. Our instincts recognize the need to shield and protect our relationship but we won't destroy each other in the process. We're not children. We're adults and we have the intelligence to know what constitutes a healthy possessiveness and what doesn't. For God's sake, trust yourself and trust me!"

Calla pressed her face into the hair-roughened, smoothly muscled chest and blinked back the tears with a sense of incredulous relief and wonder. She felt the warm protection of his arms and knew she wanted to nestle there for the rest of her life. It was right. It was what she wanted. This time she was safe.

"I'm sorry I pushed you into the pool," she mumbled against his skin a moment later and felt the quiver of deep laughter in his chest.

"If you hadn't pushed me, I probably would have pushed you. I was getting fairly near my wits' end, too! We needed something to catalyze the situation." He hugged her closer and Calla wound her arms around his waist. "Besides, I probably had it coming for the way I've been gloating all evening!"

"Gloating!"

"Certainly. Every time I saw the fire beneath the seas threatening to flame out of control, I congratulated myself again on the clever way I was using poor Brenda!"

"Brute."

"For using Brenda?"

"No, for tormenting me!"

"Ah, well, you were using Ramsey pretty effectively, too," Slade pointed out blandly.

"You didn't appear to rise to the bait," she accused, thinking that other than a few scalding glances, Slade hadn't done much about getting rid of Vance Ramsey.

"I had my mind on a higher goal this evening," he chuckled.

"Did you plan it all before you arrived?" Calla muttered, beginning to feel a little victimized.

"No, I followed you down here out of sheer instinct and because I was feeling wretched about having been so cruel to you this morning," he sighed.

"Yes, you were rather cruel," Calla agreed with alacrity, remembering how devastated she had been.

He ignored that. "Then, when Brenda appeared, I saw the look in your eyes and suddenly it seemed like too good an opportunity to miss. I decided to see if I could fan the flames."

"Well, I'm glad you enjoyed yourself earlier this evening because that was the last of the fun and games I'm going to allow tonight," Calla told him spiritedly, smiling to herself.

He bent his head to nuzzle the tip of her ear and his hands moved softly, tantalizingly along the line of her spine.

"Meaning?" he murmured unconcernedly.

"Meaning I think, now that we've ironed out the chief

problems this evening, it's time you went back to your room."

The fingers on her spine halted and she sensed the stiffening of his body.

"Are you teasing me?" he asked carefully.

"Not at all."

"Then what are you talking about, for God's sake? I have no intention of leaving you alone tonight and you know it!"

"I learned my lesson last night, Slade," Calla said demurely, pulling away from him to meet his eyes with gentle determination.

"My God!" he breathed, looking stricken. "Don't tell me you're afraid I'm going to change my mind about marrying you! I've explained to you what I was trying to do this morning! Calla, sweetheart, you must realize I have no choice but to marry you. You're a part of me! I want you fully committed to me and no one else! Don't you understand?"

"That's lovely to hear, of course, but it's not what I was worried about." She grinned impishly. "Don't let me stop you, however; a woman likes to hear that sort of declaration . . . !"

He brushed that off, determined to get to the root of the problem. "Then why won't you let me stay tonight?" he growled softly, lifting his hands to cup her face. "Honey, deep down you're not still afraid of me, are you? Afraid I'll lapse back into treating you the way I did that night after the party at the country club? Please believe me, I won't ever frighten you again. . . ."

Calla's mouth quirked slightly as she gazed up into his earnest face. Didn't he understand? She was going to have to push a little harder.

"Last night I learned there was an element of power in

204

a physical relationship," she began carefully, wondering how to put it into words. "And I decided I liked it."

"The power or the sex?" he murmured, his mouth curving.

"Both," she said lightly. "But tonight I've decided I'm going to experiment a bit with the power."

The amber eyes slitted. "Are you telling me," he said slowly, with great perception, "that because you've learned you have power over me you're going to use it?"

"Why not? Do you have any idea what a marvelous feeling it is to know that I can control you? To know that you'll do as I say even if it means taking another midnight swim to cool yourself off? You were right earlier when you told Brenda and Vance that a little taste of power can go to a woman's head! I like it. I love it! It's an element of my nature that so far I've only indulged in the business world and in my dancing. Now I'm going to extend it into whole new territory! I'll . . ."

"I *have* created a monster!" Slade exclaimed.

Calla's eyes danced with a mischief she barely concealed behind her long lashes. "Don't worry, darling Slade, as soon as we're married I'll carry you off to bed again, but until then, I'm going to find out what it's like watching a man wriggle in a woman's net."

Something very male and rather primitive coalesced in Slade's gleaming golden-brown gaze and his hands on either side of her face tightened.

"I can't figure out," he said with that dangerously neutral voice, "if you're serious or if you're teasing me. But I can guarantee that by the time tonight is over, it won't much matter. I have no intention of going back to my room."

CHAPTER TWELVE

Nimbly, Calla slipped out of his hold and out of immediate range. She turned to face him from a safe distance and smiled pointedly.

"Good night, Slade. I'll meet you for breakfast in the morning. The first lecture is at eight-thirty and since both of us are tired . . ."

"Calla, honey," he ordered roughly, "stop teasing me."

"What makes you think I'm teasing?" she mocked softly. "I'm quite serious. If you go back to your room dressed like that anyone who sees you will assume you're properly attired in a bathing suit under that towel. No one will call the house detective!"

"Come here, you little she-devil," he commanded, not moving.

"You're mixed up, Slade," Calla whispered throatily, her eyes full of deep feminine challenge. "I'm the one giving the orders tonight, remember? You wouldn't want to make me think you were going to resort to the force you displayed that night after you brought me home from the country club, would you?"

"You're really asking for it and I can't quite figure out why," he gritted, closing the distance between them with a slow stalk.

She could see the confusion in him but the determination was quickly pushing it aside, and Calla could have laughed. Her body tingled with the excitement beginning to flare in the room.

"I'm not in the mood for this," she began imperiously, and then had to slip back out of reach again as he drew too close.

"Surprisingly enough, your moods aren't my chief concern at the moment," he remarked, making another swift grab for her.

Calla tried to dodge again but this time she was too slow. His fingers closed around her waist and she was dragged into his arms. Instantly she splayed her fingers across his naked chest, pushing at him with royal disdain.

"Let me go, Slade!"

Holding her tightly with one hand, he thrust the other through the sleek knot of her hair, sending pins flying to the carpet. Then he used the loosened bronzed stuff to anchor her still further.

"I can't let you go. Even if there was a good reason for it, which there isn't!" he muttered with savage feeling. And then his mouth closed over hers.

It was a kiss of passion that nevertheless contained all, if not more than, the elemental male dominance that had exploded around her that night at the country club and later in her apartment.

It was what Calla had been looking for when she'd begun the teasing but for just an instant she questioned whether she had truly understood what she was unleashing.

But it was much too late to halt it now. Slade's mouth burned hers open, his tongue leaping into the heated depths of her mouth and claiming it. As if he had decided to waste no time on the gentle preliminaries, his fingers went to the nape of her neck, unfastening the halter of the black dress and letting it fall to her waist.

Even as she instinctively tried to grab the bodice to her breasts he had cradled her in the crook of his arm, her head on his shoulder and his free hand palming her nipples.

"Slade, wait, I didn't . . ."

Calla began the muffled protest with some breathless

208

idea of explaining but he gave her no chance. His mouth silenced hers primitively, effectively, and she knew from the tautened feel of his lean, hard length that he wasn't interested in explanations just then.

She shivered violently as his fingers moved like rough velvet over her breasts, eliciting the response they were waiting to give. She heard him groan in mounting desire as he felt the nipples harden beneath his touch.

"God, Calla!" he got out savagely. "Whatever made you think that after last night I would let you sleep alone again? Maybe you were so busy learning how to claim me that you didn't realize I was staking my claim on you! Well, there won't be any doubt in your mind after tonight!"

"Slade, listen to me, I was only . . ."

"Shut up, darling," he advised dryly, swinging her into his arms and carrying her toward the bed, "and pay attention. I'm going to give you another lesson in the relationship between sex and power!"

"Are you threatening me?" Calla demanded indignantly, her pulses racing as he dumped her lightly onto the center of the bed.

"How did you guess?" he asked admiringly, undoing the knotted towel and letting it fall unheeded to the floor.

Calla drew in her breath at the sheer male beauty of him and fell back as he came down heavily beside her, half sprawled across her softness.

"Last night you found out you could make me and yourself respond. Tonight we'll take it a step further and you'll find out that I can make you respond. That your body was made for me and it's time it acknowledged its master!"

"Master!" she gulped. "Slade, what's gotten into you? I'm not about to . . ."

The words ended on a small squeak as he yanked the

black dress all the way off and then inserted his fingers under the elastic of her silky panties. An instant later she was as naked as he, her quivering body vulnerable and burning for his touch.

"My sweet, strong, Calla," he grated, lowering his head to the valley between her small breasts. "You're mine, don't you know that? You've been mine since the first moment I saw you. It was only a matter of time before I took what belonged to me!"

She heard the arrogant masculine power and certainty in him and suddenly knew how much he had been restraining himself during the past few days of "courtship."

He was going to revel in the power he had over her, just as she had done in reverse last night. Calla moaned aloud as his teeth sank into a soft nibbling circle around one nipple.

"Slade, oh, my darling Slade!"

As if his name on her lips was a reward he had been seeking, Slade lifted his head for a long moment to stare down into her heavy-lidded eyes.

"Would you still send me back to my room if you could?" he charged.

"Damn you! You're not going to have everything your own way!" she managed faintly, knowing she was wrong.

"Yes, I am, little one," he grinned arrogantly. "I'm going to have everything I want tonight. Including the one thing you have yet to give me!"

His lips began a trail of passionate biting little kisses down the slope of her breast to the middle of her stomach and Calla's fingers closed convulsively in his dark hair.

"Oh!"

His fingers scored gently across her thighs, flickering to the inside with short, arousing little forays that brought forth shiver after shiver from Calla's body. Her legs shifted restlessly against the coverlet and her hands began to knead the muscles of his shoulders.

His tongue jabbed wetly at her navel and she cried out softly. Then she was pulled against him so that she lay on her side.

"You have the strength and suppleness of a cat and I want to own every inch of you!" he growled against the nape of her neck as her head buried itself in his shoulder.

Her lips were seeking the tanned throat when she felt his hand slide down her back, pausing at the sensitive area at the base of her spine before prowling on to clench the curve of her hip.

The tiny sting of his fingers made her arch involuntarily against him, her body seeking the aroused warmth of his. She felt the rigid tension of his spine as his maleness reacted to her.

Then his mouth was on her shoulder, exploring the curve of her throat and the erotically responsive skin behind her ear. His hands never stopped and Calla felt her senses begin to whirl in faster and faster circles.

"Oh, please, please, Slade!"

"What is it you want, little one?" he rasped, his tongue on the smooth skin of her shoulder again.

"You know I only want you. All of you!"

"Is that a cry of surrender?" he mocked gently, his leg moving to trap hers.

"Surrender!" she gasped.

"Umm. That's one of the things I'm after tonight, didn't you realize?"

"Slade, stop teasing me!" she pleaded urgently, digging her nails into his shoulders.

"But I'm not teasing you," he whispered thickly against her skin. "I'm very serious!"

"Call it anything you like, but please, please love me!"

"I will," he agreed, lifting his head once again to stare

hungrily down into her face. "If you'll love me." The tension in him was palpable.

She blinked uncertainly for an instant.

"I've loved you for days," she whispered huskily, her hands spearing through his hair in desperate little movements. "Probably since the month of the negotiations. My God! How I love you!"

"You never said it," he breathed, bending to brush her lips with a reverent touch that told her all she needed to know.

"Don't tell me you didn't realize it!" she murmured provocatively, delight singing through her body. "I thought you understood me so well!"

"Some things have to be said!" he admitted thickly.

"Then it's time you said it," she smiled with feminine invitation.

"I love you. I've loved you from the first. Just like I've wanted you from the first. For me it's all bound up together. My love and my need and my passion are inseparable. I love you, I need you, I must have you in order to go on living anything resembling a normal life. Do you understand, sweetheart?"

"Oh, yes, Slade," Calla whispered lovingly, her eyes gleaming like warm, tropical seas, "I understand. Because it is exactly the same for me. I never thought it could be this way."

He moved, forcing a space for himself between her legs with an aggressive, wholly masculine urgency, and gathered her close to him.

"Now that I have the surrender I wanted," he said with soft emphasis, "I shall take the prize I've won!"

"It's not a surrender, dammit . . . !" Calla tried to say and then her protest was shattered like fragile crystal as he claimed her with all the power of his body and his mind.

"Slade!"

After that she could no longer think coherently enough to remember her faint attempt at protest. Her body reveled in his embrace, longing to please and be pleased and achieving both goals with astonishing power.

Her hands slipped along the tensed contours of his back, down to his waist and beyond. She felt the surging rhythm catch her senses and whirl them into a raging storm of passion.

Again and again she cried out her love for him and heard him match each cry with one of his own. The fierce groans tore through his hard body and escaped from the lips buried in her throat.

Calla was lost in a wonderland of sensation and passion with only the rock of Slade's strength to cling to. Desperately she held on, thrilling to the power and primitive abandon of it all. She was his and he was hers. They belonged to each other on every level and each level reinforced another.

The combined strength pulled them into a vortex from which neither could escape, flung them to the top and over the edge of passion into the momentary darkness beyond. She heard her name called in defiant wonder.

Calla came slowly out of the suspended moment in time, aware first of the feel of Slade's arms and legs tangled with her own, holding her locked to him even in the languid aftermath of their love.

"Satisfied with your tamed monster?" she chuckled with feminine certainty. She moved her leg lazily along his until he stopped the small teasing with a clamping ankle.

"I fear it's going to be a lifetime task keeping you safely under control," he groaned lovingly, his lips in her hair. "Love me?"

"Don't tell me you still have doubts?" she mocked.

"No, I just like to hear it."

"I love you." Calla stretched boldly, letting her nipples scrape softly against his chest. "I love you, I love you, I love you!"

"Good," he retorted, sounding pleased. "Now tell me why you did it."

"Did what?" she asked innocently.

"You keep forgetting. After that month at the negotiating table, I know how your mind works. Why did you push me back into the super macho role this evening?"

"Push you? I thought you fell back into it like a second skin!"

"Thanks!" he muttered. "I'll admit it comes a little too easily around you but I've spent days teaching you what it's like to be the aggressor. And you admitted you liked it. So why did you push your luck tonight?"

She smiled dreamily up into his searching eyes, lifting a hand to toy with the tangled coffee-colored hair. "If you'd let me explain when I tried . . ."

"Things had gone a little too far for explanations at that point," he pointed out dryly.

"Yes, well, my reasoning process was simple enough. I only wanted you to know you didn't have to keep on restraining yourself around me. I didn't want you to think I really needed to be treated like fine china all the time!"

He laughed ruefully, hugging her close for a moment. "You little idiot. I'm not sure I like the idea of you manipulating me like that!"

"From now on you'll never be quite sure, will you?" she teased.

He muttered something semi-violent that conveyed extreme masculine frustration.

"You ought to know by now I can hold my own with you," he reminded her with a touch of familiar arrogance. Then he relented. "All the same, I'm glad you weren't really frightened that night when I used the judo on you.

214

I spent one hell of a bad night worrying that I'd ruined my chances completely! You even reduced me to resorting to blackmail! I was never so relieved about anything in my life as I was when I got you to agree to let me court you!"

"I was pretty relieved myself!" she admitted cheerfully.

"Umm?"

"Well, I was worrying about how I was going to keep you at arm's length for another three months, and I thought that if you were involved with a more routine sort of courtship I might be able to control the situation a little better."

"I thought that was probably it, but I didn't give a damn. I figured anything that made you see me frequently was worth a try."

"What would you have done if I'd refused the court-ship?"

"Found one excuse after another to see you at work and kept you late at the office as often as possible. Sooner or later I figured you'd get a chance to taste my cooking and you'd be hooked! I was counting on that or the soaring to make you my slave for life."

"A winning combination," she murmured.

"Both of which we could have enjoyed this weekend," he felt obliged to point out, "if you hadn't raced off in a huff this afternoon!"

"Oh, good grief!"

"What's the matter?"

"I just remembered Brenda and Vance! They must be wondering what in the world became of us!" Calla grinned.

"I think between the two of them they'll be able to figure it out," Slade muttered disinterestedly. "Now, about your plans for this weekend . . ."

"Yes, Mr. York?"

"I'm going to suggest a change of itinerary," he began purposefully.

"You mean you don't want to view the MATS display or hear the lecture on Quality Circles?" she asked, wide-eyed.

"I would much prefer to discuss plans for a honeymoon that has already been delayed for over a month!"

"There's a coffee break scheduled for ten o'clock, right after the first of the morning lectures. We could probably find time to discuss it then."

"Silly female," he whispered affectionately, his eyes warm and golden in lazy appraisal. "Haven't we just established how well-suited I am to play the dominating male role? You're out of your tiny little mind if you think I'm going to spend the next two days sitting through a series of seminars on the latest in instrumentation!"

"You're going to go back to Phoenix and wait for me to return on Sunday night?"

"I'm going to strap you in behind the wheel of that Fiat of yours first thing in the morning and then I'm going to point you in the right direction and follow you home to make sure you do as you're told!"

"And when we get home?"

"Then I'll take you soaring and stuff you full of the best lasagna you've ever tasted!" he told her in no uncertain terms. "After that we'll go soaring again."

"Again?"

"This time we won't need to bother with a sailplane."

"Oh, I see."

"I thought you would," he told her smugly and lowered his head once again to the honey of her mouth.

Less than a week later Calla turned lazily in her lounger, gold flashing from the circlet on her left hand, and murmured sleepily, "Here we are by a pool again."

"Well, what do you expect?" Slade offered philosophically, reaching out to grasp her hand without bothering to open his eyes. "Phoenix has an awful lot of them. This *is* the Valley of the Sun, you know."

"I know, but I'm beginning to think there may be something symbolic in all of it."

"At least this time it's my pool," he chuckled with satisfaction. "Lots of privacy."

"Just the place for a business discussion," Calla agreed.

"We're supposed to be on a honeymoon," he reminded her in a sardonic drawl.

"Yes, I know, that's why I'm initiating the discussion. Men are supposed to be at their most amenable while they're on honeymoons."

"You're going to bring up those Quality Circles again, aren't you?" he demanded with great wariness.

"How did you guess?"

"This isn't very fair of you, Calla," he pointed out reproachfully, using his free hand to reach for the glass of lemonade. The amber eyes flickered open watchfully as he sipped the cool drink.

"You don't expect a silly argument like that to stop me, do you?"

"No," he sighed.

"I want six more months' trial with them, Slade," she said in no-nonsense tones.

"We agreed to three."

"That's not long enough. They had just gotten off the ground when you took over Chapman, Inc. Six months is the least amount of time you should allow for the experiment."

He shut his eyes against the sun, the long lashes moving seductively on his high cheekbones. "What do I get if I let you have six months?"

"You'll get a more loyal, more efficient work force!" she

217

declared stoutly, warming to her theme. "And much improved quality control!"

"Not good enough. I can get that in other ways."

She hesitated. "What do you want in return for the six months?"

"Let's see. I want a guarantee of full management cooperation in implementing those new cost-cutting proposals I'm having prepared . . ."

"Impossible! Some of those proposals would cost twice as much to implement as they're designed to save. The workload on the secretaries alone would make many of them pointless. Our staff doesn't have time for the kind of paper trial your high-priced consultant suggested!"

"His ideas deserve the same kind of trial you're demanding for the QCs!" Slade argued firmly.

"All right! Six months for six months! And at the end of that time I'm going to take great pleasure in pointing out that my six months produced a much more important improvement in the company than your six months did!"

"I'm sure you will," he agreed soothingly.

"Why are you smiling like that?" Calla demanded suspiciously

"No particular reason."

"Oh, yes there is, and I want to hear it!" She pulled an ice cube out of her glass and dropped it on his bare, sun-warmed stomach. ·

"What the hell!" Slade sat up with a start, reaching for her vengefully.

But Calla was already on her feet, heading for the relative safety of the pool.

"Come back here, you little . . . !"

In an instant he was cleaving the water behind her, catching her ankle as she darted away. Calla was hauled unceremoniously back toward him through the blue-green liquid.

"Now," he declared with anticipation, "you're going to pay for that unwarranted attack on my person!"

He dunked her firmly and then pulled her up against him, watching in open amusement as she sputtered and caught her breath. She clamped her arms around his neck.

"I'll pull you under with me if you do that again!" she warned.

"A stand-off," he grinned.

"Tell me why you were smiling, Slade York!" she commanded, laughing up at him.

"Can't you guess?" he taunted.

"Knowing you there could have been any one of a number of evil reasons!"

"It was because you'd just managed to negotiate yourself into staying on my payroll for six months instead of three," he told her complacently.

"Oh!"

"Neat, huh?"

"You planned it?" she asked, with patently false admiration. Her fingers began making patterns on his streaming shoulders.

"Let's say I've been waiting for the appropriate opportunity."

"I suppose your ability to maneuver people like that is one of the reasons you're my boss," she murmured ingenuously.

"Probably," he agreed, his fingers slipping inside the top of the green maillot swimsuit as the amber eyes flamed.

"Keep in mind that seven years from now when I'm thirty-seven I shall have a great deal more experience at this sort of negotiating. You won't find me such an easy mark!"

"Yes, ma'am," he agreed politely, skimming the wet suit off her body with a swift two-handed movement.

219

"Slade!" she protested automatically, finding herself deliciously nude in the water. Inwardly she was smiling complacently at the knowledge that her husband would never see her as a threat no matter how successful she became in her own right. But there were other things in life now besides success. . . . Her shimmering eyes were full of love when she looked up at him.

"Remember that no matter how old you get I'm always going to have seven more years of experience," he warned, arching her slick, pliant body into his own and lowering his mouth to hers.

"It won't help you," she promised wickedly. "I'm a fast learner and a born negotiator. We'll see who's running York Instruments seven years from now!" Blissfully she condemned herself to years instead of months on the company payroll.

"You're planning on banishing me to the kitchen?" he asked laughingly against her mouth.

"I think you're happiest there," she told him kindly.

"Not quite. This is where I'm happiest!" he declared firmly and claimed her mouth completely.

LOOK FOR NEXT MONTH'S
CANDLELIGHT ECSTASY ROMANCES™:

Dell Bestsellers

☐ **NOBLE HOUSE** by James Clavell.............$5.95 (16483-4)
☐ **PAPER MONEY** by Adam Smith.................$3.95 (16891-0)
☐ **CATHEDRAL** by Nelson De Mille...............$3.95 (11620-1)
☐ **YANKEE** by Dana Fuller Ross....................$3.50 (19841-0)
☐ **LOVE, DAD** by Evan Hunter......................$3.95 (14998-3)
☐ **WILD WIND WESTWARD**
   by Vanessa Royal.....................................$3.50 (19363-X)
☐ **A PERFECT STRANGER**
   by Danielle Steel.......................................$3.50 (17221-7)
☐ **FEED YOUR KIDS RIGHT**
   by Lendon Smith, M.D. $3.50 (12706-8)
☐ **THE FOUNDING**
   by Cynthia Harrod-Eagles...........................$3.50 (12677-0)
☐ **GOODBYE, DARKNESS**
   by William Manchester...............................$3.95 (13110-3)
☐ **GENESIS** by W.A. Harbinson.....................$3.50 (12832-3)
☐ **FAULT LINES** by James Carroll $3.50 (12436-0)
☐ **MORTAL FRIENDS** by James Carroll $3.95 (15790-0)
☐ **THE SOLID GOLD CIRCLE**
   by Sheila Schwartz.....................................$3.50 (18156-9)
☐ **AMERICAN CAESAR**
   by William Manchester...............................$4.50 (10424-6)

At your local bookstore or use this handy coupon for ordering:

Dell DELL BOOKS
P.O. BOX 1000, PINE BROOK, N.J. 07058-1000

Please send me the books I have checked above. I am enclosing $_____ (please add 75c per copy to cover postage and handling). Send check or money order—no cash or C.O.D.'s. Please allow up to 8 weeks for shipment.

Mr./Mrs./Miss_____

Address_____

City_____ State/Zip_____